PRIYARANJAN KUMAR

Tales Of Sales

Fun, Factual and Fundamental

15 Simple Solutions for Complicated Situations

BLUEROSE PUBLISHERS
India | U.K.

For permissions requests or inquiries regarding this publication, please contact:

BLUEROSE PUBLISHERS
www.BlueRoseONE.com
info@bluerosepublishers.com
+91 8882 898 898
+4407342408967

ISBN: 978-93-5989-981-7

Cover design: Shivam
Typesetting: Namrata Saini

First Edition: December 2023

To My Fellow Sales men/women

for the love, affection and respect
you always showered upon me across organizations !

To My Family

for the sacrifices and encouragement
you stood like a rock behind me every time unconditionally !

Preface

It was the April of 2020, when India was reeling in the horror of Covid-19. Everyone that I spoke to was shaky, uncertain and fearful about the future. Jobs and lives were at stake. Few of my acquaintances reached out for help with hospital admissions which I tried to help to the best of my ability and contacts. All through I was hearing sorrowful stories of people, putting me under depression. I was getting sucked into a cycle of disappointment and despondency along with paranoia with each passing day. Then one day I decided to end this vicious cycle and the best way I decided was to write. But write what, for whom and why? I was shy, inhibited and introverted to express myself freely but somehow I got the strength to break this shackles and started sharing my thoughts on Retail Management on LinkedIn. After a couple of posts I realized that people started liking the content I was posting. It was cathartic to me as I started coming out of my depressed state of mind. I started to write more anecdotal and observatory stuff on LinkedIn and got more appreciation.

The best responses that I received were for a story I posted about my work with Mars Chocolates and establishing the Sales and Distribution in the suburb of Indirapuram in Ghaziabad. I decided to pen down the complete incident and saved it. Couple of years later while I continued to write extensively on LinkedIn on specific subjects of Retail Management, Sales &

Distribution, FMCG, Leadership and Organizational Behaviour, someone commented on the post I had penned down. The idea of writing "Tales of Sales" germinated from there as I could sense that people appreciated genuine content and there is no other better way of expressing oneself apart from a story. But penning down 300 words is completely different from writing a book. The book had to be coherent and relatable to the readers, so I decided to base it on stories but with a twist. Each story had to be connected with one essential attribute required in the field of doing real sales on the ground.

I went back in my eighteen years of career and life to zero down on fifteen such qualities which have helped me. After I finalized those, the next step was to go hunting my memory structure to recall incidents, events and situations which could be best exemplified with these attributes. I wrote the first story which was the hardest as I was not able to write more than a page. I reworked and rethought the same and then came up with an extensive version of the same. Chapter 1 was completed which to the next to the next and finally putting the full stop on the fifteenth Chapter.

While the actual time taken from start to finish may have been six months but this is eighteen years of pure unadulterated learnings and experiences. Considering the sensitivities regarding identification of some characters in my stories, names have been changed.

Show some love and Happy Reading !
Priyaranjan

Contents

Relationships 1

Transparency 8

Adaptability 16

Tenacity 23

Learning 30

Risk 37

Acceptability 45

Responsibility 51

Engagement 59

Passion 66

Fortitude 73

Audacity 82

Rationality 89

Improvisation 96

Fearless 104

Relationships!

Delhi. October 2012

Winter was about to set in, the weather was fabulous. Delhi is at its best during this time of the year when it is neither unbearably hot nor bone-chilling cold. There is a general feeling of bonhomie & warmth in this season.

It was a chilly Saturday morning when I reached the shopping capital of Delhi & arguably one of the most famous spots in the Capital of India, Connaught Place. I parked my Silver Ford Ikon in front of Hanuman Temple & walked with an element of uncertainty in my head.

I saw a group of 10 grown up men waiting for me with an air of expectation & anxiety. I signalled to them to assemble at Coffee House, one of the landmark locations of Connaught Place. They quickly started to group the tables & chairs to make it a long table. All of them took their places while I sat at the head of the table. "Filter Coffee & Bun Maska for everyone" I told the waiter. Coffee House is synonymous for Sales Meetings & Mini Performance Reviews but everyone around was surprised as I pulled out Class VIII book on

Mathematics. I was about to teach Profit & Loss, Fractions today to these 30+ pot-bellied Men who were behaving like they had been sent back to school.

The back story starts in the last week of April 2010. I was desperately looking for a job opportunity in order to exit my current assignment as the Branch Sales Manager Haryana with United Breweries. The stress of Overdue Collections from Liquor wholesalers was extremely painful. I had got used to playing the waiting game at the wholesalers points, which was tiring me out. One day, I could not handle the wait any longer, so in order to beat the stress, decided to take a cat nap at a Petrol Pump owned by cricketer Chetan Sharma on Faridabad Gurgaon Road in my Air-Conditioned Ford IKON on a blistering hot April day.

My phone beeped, those days were such that any call starting 0124-4xxxxxx was important for me as it would most likely be from a Job Consultant. I was woken up from my slumber, "Hello, Priyaranjan, I'm Nisha from Synergy. Are you looking for a job change?". I would have said "Yes" at least five times in 3 seconds. She explained the role to me which, I did not even hear. I said, "I'm interested". After a couple of rounds of Interview in Gurgaon & Hyderabad, I had got my offer letter and my freedom pass from the living hell.

The 14th of June 2010 was special as I tried to locate an address in Okhla Industrial Area phase 1 in non-Google Map days. I joined the Business Team of Mars Inc (one of the biggest Confectionary brands in the world) as Sales Operations Manager. Mars was looking at building the Chocolate Business in India, offering mega brands Snickers, Mars, Galaxy, Twix & Bounty to the Indian Consumer. The only way to reach the refrigerator of this Consumer was to build an expansive Sales and distribution network across the country. I was tasked to accomplish this in North & East India. Starting a business from scratch is always extremely tough & in order to progress it was imperative to put boots on the ground. Therefore, I started to hire the Front Line Sales Team.

I handpicked them for their experience, attitude & Relationships they had built with the Retailers because it was important to occupy Cash Tills at Retailer points in order to drive Impulse buying of Chocolates. The Front-End Team was extremely motivated & passionate in capturing Cash Tills but all of them lacked a proper Graduation degree. They had risen up the ranks with their ability & hard work over many years.

We had hired them on 3rd party Payroll which was a big irritant to them as all of them wanted the Mars payroll. The challenge in taking them on roll was their absence of basic Educational Qualification.

But all of them did a fabulous job. Distribution scaled up exponentially & so did the Sales. The Organization was growing with an expectation to deliver Growths Month on Month which meant bigger distribution & a greater number of People. After a year the Management decided to professionalise this layer of Front End & get them on board as Full-Time Employees on Mars payroll. It was easy to hire from outside, but it created a disparity in the ecosystem demoralising the engine of a revving sales machine.

Some people believed that Smarter & better qualified Sales Officers would be able to scale this business up quickly on the lines of any large FMCG company in India. The implicit understanding was that they would be better with analysis & numbers, which was required as the complexity in business was increasing. The Current lot knew how to sell, capture cash tills, occupy chiller space, put up Retailer Boards, install Visi Coolers but they were clueless with data interpretation, logical reasoning & arithmetic. I was extremely uncomfortable with this change management as I knew deep down that it would disturb the complete apple cart.

I convinced the Management to give these guys called RANKERS a fair chance. They relented & declared a date for Aptitude Test & Personal Interview. These guys were rocking with everything else but were rocked by this declaration because they knew they would not be able to open their account in the Test. All ten of them were crestfallen. The world had come crashing down on them hitting their dreams & aspirations very hard. Dejected & disappointed, they met me one evening in Noida with tears in their eyes. “Sir, you are our only hope. We have learnt so much from you. Please help us”, said a couple of them in unison.

I was overcome with emotion & in that moment, made an inexplicable decision. I don’t know what struck me but I told them, “I would make you ready in 21 days”. Bewildered, all of them looked at each other & then at me with their eyes wide open not knowing what was going through my head. The scene from Bollywood movie "Lagaan" was playing out in real life where ragtag team of 11 guys who had never played cricket or touched a bat & ball were challenging the cricket playing Englishmen to save their lives & livelihood.

So, the learning trek started with meetings every second day in the Evening or Morning at United Coffee House Connaught Place & I would teach them basic Mathematics, Algebra, Geometry, Logical Reasoning. It was probably the toughest task of my life till then. Hours would go, endless cups of coffee & bread toast ordered, but to make them understand was like trying to cycle in a cyclone. "Have I done the right thing? Have I given them false hope?" I would question myself at least twice every day. I felt weighed down by the sheer weight of the hope & expectations which these people had placed on me.

But I badgered on, sometimes lovingly, sometimes angry, sometimes joyfully. Days were passing rapidly & then it was only 3 days to go for D-Day. After a gruelling 3-4 Hour every second day Sessions, I was able to see a faint light of hope emerging Majority of them had caught up on the concepts & had begun to get the basic step calculations correct. Percentages, Profit Loss, Relationship Trees, Fractions etc, we had covered a lot. In the last 3 days, I prepared them for the Interview on how to introduce themselves, their family, achievements, and career goals, areas of improvement, team handling & Situation Behaviour Impact (SBI) Scenarios. They meticulously noted down everything, like Primary School Kids would note down their homework for the day.

I was nervous like hell on the day they were writing their test & appearing for interviews. I was explaining concepts till last minute before the test would start. It is often said, hard work never ever goes waste. All those hours spent in Coffee House bore fruit as all of them but one made it through to be rightfully given the On Roll Designation of Sales Officers & Benefits of Full Time Employee.

I was overjoyed with their achievement. It felt like I had achieved something special in my life. There is no greater joy than to see your own people climb the ladder of success in life. This is probably the reason why teaching is considered such a noble profession.

Years rolled by, and I had moved on from Mars. A couple of them always made a point to call me on my Birthday & Diwali reminiscing about the days I was leading them. I had completely forgotten about most parts of my tenure at Mars when couple of days back I saw "Surender Calling" flashing on my mobile screen.

"Namaste Sir, how are you?" said Surender. I could immediately recognize his baritone voice. After exchanging pleasantries, I asked him about his current location & news about his life.

"Sir, I called you to let you know that I have been awarded as the Best Sales Officer for this year." I congratulated him & asked him about his family. He had been able to build a house for his family in Uttarakhand, get his elder daughter married & younger one admitted in MBBS Course. He choked while he thanked me profusely for those sessions at Coffee House. "Sir, *aap nahi hote to yeh na hota*". If you were not there, this would not have happened.

I smiled recollecting that I fought probably the hardest for Surender because I believed his talent & potential did not depend on one educational degree.

It felt nice as I had made a difference. I had built relationships for life!

Moral of the Story: Building a career is all about building relationships. It is the cornerstone of one's success. Therefore there should always be extra effort to build positive interactions.

Transparency!

Gurgaon. June 2009

It had been around 4 Months since I had been selling Kingfisher Beer in Rural & Urban Haryana. I was designated as the Branch Sales Manager & was responsible for Market Share, Sales & Collection of United Breweries brands in the state. The brand 'Kingfisher' was iconic with its surrogate advertising happening through Kingfisher Airlines, Kingfisher Formula 1, Kingfisher Calendar & the newly minted Indian Premier League in cricket.

From the outside it looked a glamourous job to the extent that I was naïve in not even negotiating for the salary & saying "It is a dream company. The role matters & not the money'. Hindsight it was the most foolish statement to make. My first day was nothing short of horrifying. I joined the United Breweries Regional Office of North 1 territory situated at Bikaji Cama Place New Delhi in early March of 2009. The first day at a new job sets the tone for the tenure however for me it upset the tone at the very start. I was made to wait for the entire day in front of non-functioning desktop in a small cubicle barely enough to fit in my body frame listening to the yelling with the choicest of North Indian abuses. I waited & waited till evening 5pm when the Regional Head called me to his chamber. Meanwhile he commanded his orderly to get something from his car. The help walked in with a packet & put it on his table. The Regional Head checked the packet, opened the chest drawer & put a shiny silver coloured pistol. I was shocked & asked him a stupid question: "Sir, why do you need this?"

"It is for my personal safety" he said. I was trembling with the days proceedings & kicking myself to pick something up like this without consulting anyone.

The next few days I was despatched to badlands of Haryana. Those days I used to live in Indirapuram, Ghaziabad, I took a taxi ride from Ghaziabad to Sirsa. "Where should I reach?" I asked Deepak, the Territory Sales Executive for Hissar belt. "Sir, Ranbir Singh Godara". The name sounded royal & regal but the place was complete anti thesis to royalty.

I entered the massive gates into a compound to see three White Scorpios & Bolero's with three charpoys in middle of the compound. Four massively built men with twirling moustaches were sharing a long winding hookah. Deepak bowed down in respect to touch their feet while I stood erect saying "Namaste". "Brother" in chaste Haryanvi dialect, the main man Ranbir Singh Godara said "when will you send the Beer, My L2's (Liqour vends are stocked out with Kingfisher". "Sir, you have an Overdue" Deepak stuttered. We are not running away. Turning to me he said "Listen, you send me the beer, I will make old payment but first send me the beer".

I could only mumble in response learning my first lesson on the field to be prepared with data for any meeting. It was real hostile bowling in typical English conditions which I was facing as an Indian batsmen. But like in Test Cricket, the first session is always the toughest to negotiate, I had done reasonably in handling the initial couple of months.

As time rolled by, I decided to take the bull by its horns, so I started getting used to the Restrictive Distribution of Beer as well as the high-handedness of the Channel partners. The balance of power was completely in the hands of the wholesalers. While I was struggling with the situation & trying to come to terms with it, unknown to me there was a new challenge brewing up. IPL was a new entity in the Cricket-Entertainment World. The 1st edition was a roaring success with the glitz & glamour of Bollywood & Cheerleaders. Brands which could afford this asset to advertise were lapping it up & Kingfisher was one of them. Since it could only do surrogate advertising, IPL was a great platform for the brand to advertise.

Divided by Teams, United by Kingfisher was the in thing as the Kingfisher Bird logo was being sported by Royal Challengers Bangalore & couple of more teams. The "oo lala le oo" jingle was constantly streaming on radios & televisions.

"Thailand". Most distributors & channel partners in India's distribution eco system are always overjoyed with this contest whenever any Organization would announce. Wholesalers & Retailers of United Breweries got even better opportunity to witness the IPL sitting in Corporate Boxes rubbing shoulders with Shahrukh

Khan & Juhi Chawla. Therefore, IPL passes demand was a big draw & constant source of irritation for me. For every One pleased person there was two displeased ones especially in the liquor trade as every Wholesaler thought he was the next to Vijay Mallya in the business.

India was to undergo General Elections in the Summer of 2009 & there was ambiguity about hosting the IPL during that time because of Security concerns. Options started to get reported of staging the IPL in phases in India or outside India with UAE emerging as the frontrunner. In midst of all speculations, Breaking News came "IPL 2nd Edition to be shifted to South Africa". The rainbow nation was about to see the Indian Corporate & Bollywood economic power over the next 45 days.

While it was a nightmare for the broadcasters, players, organizers, it was an even bigger challenge for us as we had to pick & select a few wholesalers who would travel to South Africa. When the IPL happened in India, the number of passes that could be given out were in hundreds but now we could only accommodate 15 People. My Boss, Regional Manager decided whom to take with him & I was tasked to coordinate picking up Passports & other necessary documents. The selection of the travellers was based purely on the whims of the Boss without considering basic parameters of the business.

Since I was a newbie in the industry compared to this stalwart, I trusted his decision & started to work as per instructions but deep down I knew something was amiss. As expected the news spread like wild fire within the Wholesaler community in Haryana that Kingfisher was taking people to South Africa for IPL. People who were on board the flight were extremely happy while those left behind were fuming.

Amongst the lot left behind, they vented out their anger by stopping Ordering & selling Kingfisher. What was meant to drive up Dealer Engagement, Sales & Market Share, it was proving to be counterproductive. I had to act & handle the situation because with passing day of peak Summer, we were losing Sales & Market Share badly to Haywards 5000 (SAB Miller) & Thunderbolt (Mount Shivalik), the other popular brands in the market.

Krishna Wines in Jhajjar (One of the districts in Haryana) was not placing orders resulting in loss of market share in the district. So, I decided to go & meet him. He was miffed with his name being omitted for African Safari. I drove from Ghaziabad to his Haveli in Jhajjar. I knew it would be a rough day, so was prepping up mentally with the Aamir Khan philosophy of 3 Idiots "All iz Well".

After a 2-hour long drive through the farm lands of interior Haryana, I parked my car in his premises. I was led into one of the rooms which resembled one from a rundown palace in Bollywood movies of 1970's. I sat there squirming on the Wooden Sofa expecting a tirade & volley of abuses which made my heart beat faster & faster. One hour later Not so Gentle-Man turned up resembling a Bollywood Villain from 90's Ajay Devgan Movie.

Massively built with biceps bulging & thick Gold chains & bracelet dangling from neck & wrists with Two

Bodyguards, he stared at me. The eyes were piercing & the redness conveyed clearly that I was facing a very angry Man in his den. "You idiots @#%^&**%$# decided to take XYZ from Bahadurgarh, Hissar but not me. They are kids in front of me. $%^&**!@#$, you company guys need to be taught a lesson that you will not forget". Those few minutes made me shudder before he finished his expletive strewn monologue. It seemed like an hour since he had been abusing me. I was hearing some of the expletives for the first time in my life, which for a boy coming from Western Uttar Pradesh was unbelievable.

He shouted, abused, gestured for 10 minutes with his side kicks egging him on to give me more of the same. He banged his literal Sunny Deol's Two pounder fists on the table making me supremely nervous. My mind was racing. I kept thinking, "How to stop him in his tracks?". Life Lesson that I learnt was that interjecting an angry man accentuates the anger while listening patiently douses the fire quickly. While I was standing through this tirade, I suddenly sat down on the chair. The movement broke his anger momentum. I knew he would sit down since I was sitting & while sitting he would not be able to shout & abuse as hard. This is a trick I picked up in anger management, in order to calm a very angry person, one should ask him to sit down. It is 10 times more difficult to shout once anyone is sitting.

I don't know from where but I gathered courage to chip in, "Sir, shouting & abusing will not make you more right. If you are right, you are right without high volume & choicest abuses. And if you are wrong, you will be wrong with the same high volume & choicest abuses." He was taken aback at my firm but polite tone. I had got my cue; this was the opportunity I could not afford to let go. He was quiet for a minute, maybe trying to process what I had just said or maybe wondering how this 5ft 10 inch man could open his mouth in front of him & his goons.

I had prepared few data points as I had anticipated this conversation from my first visit to Ranbir Singh Godara in Sirsa. Very quickly I showed him his purchase in the last year was only 2800 Cases of Beer while the Wholesalers who went on a Trip were all who bought 20,000 + Cases. I showed him delayed payment record with Overdue ranging from 120 days to 360 Days. My files were ready & he was taken aback with the papers that I had prepared. Then I asked him will he take any of his Retailers to a Trip to Bangkok if they had such a pitiable record. The word BANG kok is magical. It lightens any conversation quickly. The tension in the air evaporated. All of us laughed. Second Life Lesson was Data with Humour always works. Data puts the toughest & most illogical people on backfoot.

Then hectic negotiations ensued. He was adamant to deduct 1.5 Lacs Rupees from the Outstanding in lieu of the trip. I did not budge while he tried all tricks of human behaviour to change my stance. Neither did I give him any opportunity to create any ambiguity in the conversation. "I have not seen many people like you who are standing ramrod straight & not budging from your stance at all & somehow I'm not getting angry at this," said the Owner. I smiled back with folded hands.

It was already 3.00 pm. "You must have lunch with me," he said. I immediately accepted the friendly gesture. It was the first time in my life I was having typical Haryanvi village food which was freshly cooked & piping hot. Ghee & butter was dripping all over the Curry & vegetables with large chapatis getting served every minute. I ate to my hearts content.

I walked out after 4 hours of discussion, some laughs, hearty rustic jiggery dipped meal & cheques for all overdues.

Moral of the Story is Good Sales People are authentic & transparent in their conversation & body language. They do not leave any room for any confusion or miscommunication in their deliberations & negotiations.

Adaptability!

Bangalore. June 2013

My mind & heart were at loggerheads. It was the end of May 2013 in middle of a blistering heat wave that I was sitting in front of the Managing Director of Mars India (Chocolate Business) in one of the Café Coffee Day's in Gurgaon. "Tell me what I can do to hold you back" he asked. I said I don't know but right now I just want a change.

For the last two years I was having a platinum run in Mars Chocolate business in India having just received the award of the "Most Engaged Associate", Winning a Trip to China & Hong Kong & Merit Increment of 25%. It was a near perfect scenario & it would not have been unfair to think that I was the blue-eyed boy of the Organization. I was recognized, respected & rewarded sufficiently for me not look anywhere outside Mars India.

But the mind was restless. The Pepsi slogan "Yeh Dil Maange more" kept reverberating through my head all the time. I was doing the same mundane thing day after day for the last 3 years. I needed some freshness, something new & challenging. Add to it the irritants of constant supervisor changes, unproductive marathon meetings, and misunderstanding of the ground realities were adding to the confused thoughts. Amidst all of this commotion, I updated my resume after three years at naukri.com.

Soon, I got a call from Vandana, who was a Senior Recruitment Consultant with ABC Consultants offering me the position of Regional Head for South with Nivea India. Some brands are bigger in consumers mind than they actually are in real life. Nivea was one in that category of brands. I was surprised to hear about the size of the business because the Blue Tin of Nivea had been a multi-generational permanent feature in every household during the winter season. "You will be reporting to Dev. He is a veteran in the cosmetics industry," said Vandana. I looked up the credentials of Dev & Amit who was the Managing Director & was mighty impressed with their experience.

I was excited with the category of the product which was personal care & cosmetics, different from Chocolate Sales & Distribution which I had done for the last 3 years. My bigger Objective was about moving to work in a new Geography where I did not understand any of the South Indian languages. I had already spent Seven years living & working in Delhi & therefore wanted to explore South India because of the inherent differentiators of People, Consumers & Channel. It would seem counter intuitive but that was my calling. "Your meeting is fixed with Dev at Café Coffee Day in Galleria Market in Gurgaon on Saturday 6.30 pm", informed Vandana. I met Dev, answered his questions, explained my body of work & tried to understand his expectations. Quite often the basic issue of misalignment between managers & their direct reports is ambiguity in expectations. I tried my best to clearly understand what he was looking for. A couple of weeks later, I sat in front of the Managing Director repeating exactly what I said to Dev.

I have always got extremely excited with ambiguity, difficult situations, problems to the extent that I go out & look for a problem. This was a perfect match for me. Nivea as a brand is associated with the Blue Tin which is synonymous with winter season having a large portfolio of Body Lotions, Lip Balms, Creams which is the mainstay & identity for the brand. But South India, barring Bangalore & Hyderabad for few days, does not see winter as a season. It is hot, hotter, and hottest at different times of the year. Therefore, Body Lotions & Creams did not sell as much, which made Deodorant as the lead product for the brand. Deodorant in India was one of the most cluttered categories. So, I knew I was up against an unknown geography, no local language understanding & challenging product. But this was what was giving me an adrenaline rush.

Somewhere in mid-June 2013, I joined Nivea India. I was supposed to shadow the Regional Manager of North for a week in Delhi to understand the day to day operational aspects of the business. I reached Connaught Place & waited for Kuldeep to arrive on a Monday morning. As I sat on the first floor trying to kill time by fiddling with my Nokia E71 in non-Netflix & non YouTube days, I could see an Oyo like full & unabashed make out session on the couch. The passion & intensity was enough to turn my Cold Coffee into a hot one. Soon,

Kuldeep walked in & I listened to him patiently for the next couple of hours, asking some intelligent & some stupid questions. A year down, we became great friends & continue to do so till today. I worked with Sales Officer called BDO's (Business Development Officers) for next five days in the market in the grueling heat of June trying to juice out every ounce of knowledge & absorbing it as a sponge.

My next destination was the Nivea Headquarters in Mumbai. The first couple of days were spent in a 4x4 ft cubicle where the Induction meeting was happening with disinterested people from different departments were coming in & giving me a spiel. One common thread amongst all the cacophony was the supposed nonperformance of the business in South was due to the supposed incompetence of the Managers in South namely Suresh, Chandan & Jagan. They were on the firing list. I realized that people is the soft underbelly of organizational underperformance. It is extremely easy to put the blame on specific people & remove them but replacing them again with people who would face the same challenges. The focus is never on solving the real problem but on delivering some actionable by firing people.

"Take your time, make up your mind but replace them," thundered the Managing Director. I didn't know what to understand from that statement but with this background & my North Indian aggressive stints I landed in Bangalore to drive the business. I committed a cardinal mistake of acting on the prescription that I received from Mumbai which was downloaded verbatim on the team immediately with same force & pressure that works in North. The Second Mistake was to discredit my predecessor which is a life lesson. It happens all the time in most organizations at all positions starting from the CEO to the Sales Officer. The team was taken aback by my high handed approach & went into a shell. I could make out clearly that I was being treated like a total outsider who was just interested in screwing the happiness of everyone down below without bothering to understand the ground reality.

As time was passing I was getting more desperate. I was shouting more, losing my temper more & getting lesser results. A couple of months later, I realized my foolhardiness. I started to recognize that Market Context is completely different. Weather is different to other parts of India, there is no winter. It gets hot & hotter in South so Blue Tin & Allied Products become less effective. Deodorant becomes the lead category naturally which is extremely cluttered. People & Culture are very different. Turbo Charging with Expletives, Lion, Tiger & Cheetah synonyms don't work in South. It's a very logical, methodical, sober & consistent mode of leadership which people look up to. Celebrities, Language & Festivals are different in all Four States, even the Nature (Price Fluctuations General Trade vs Modern Trade) & Size of Stores (Supermarket) is unlike other parts of India.

South India is actually four different countries put together. Most Organizations fail to understand South context & they operate with North India superimposition on South. No wonder organizations which have their HQ in South are always more dominant there. I was in 3rd month of tenure in South & was getting used to Market, Distributors & Team who spoke four languages. For most North Indians, South India is like a homogenous group while fact is all four states (now five) are different from each other in Food, Language, Culture, Habits, Body Language. Idly Sambar tastes very different in Saravana Bhawan in Chennai to Sukh Sagar in Bangalore. Biryani in Hyderabad vs Biryani in Cochin is as different as chalk & cheese.

It was minor detail that I did not understand any of four languages & was all at sea. Type of retail outlets in 4 metros of South are different from each other. Bangalore was more individual supermarket, Chennai was all about huge Saravana Store & Pothy while Hyderabad was about Ratnadeep, Vijeta, Ghanshyam.

I was struggling big time with language as Distributor, Salesman, Retailer all spoke local language barring Cosmetic Stores in Bangalore who all interestingly belong to Pali in Rajasthan. Years later I heard this anecdote from a Colleague "Jahan na pahuche Gaadi, wahan bhi mile Marwaadi"

My initial market Visits to Chennai & Coimbatore were hell. I used to get regularly confused between Calicut, Kottayam, Trivandrum & found it difficult to pronounce Towns names like Pathanamthitta. I could relate so much with Shrikant Tiwari of Family Man when he regularly asks Muthu to translate Tamil. But I could not forever operate on mute mode. So, I decided to make a sales dictionary

I meticulously noted down sales lingo

Stocks Rates, Wholesale, Undercutting, Outstanding, Losses, Profit, Damages, Cheque Clear, Cheque Bounce, NEFT, Claims Settlement, Subsidy, Budget, Lazy,

Furlough, Sharp, Fool, Primary Billing, Secondary Sales, Display, Schemes, Discount, Percentage, Coverage, Visibility, Numerals, Modern Trade, Salesman, Route, Good, Horrible.

I learnt these words in all 4 languages of Kannada, Malayalam, Tamil & Telugu. I could from then on understand what anyone said as they would structure their sentences only using these words. From then onwards my acceptability to the team increased manifold. They started to see me as one of their own. The market visits became better as inadvertently while speaking the local language in front of me, team would try & translate in English. I would smile back & tell them that I have understood & they would a big smile on their face. My biggest achievement was to attend a Distributor Meet in Chennai & understand everything which was discussed there.

Though I could not speak any of the four languages but my body language became more confident & outgoing with the team. We gelled well & delivered expected results for the Organization. In fact, when I was leaving, I could not believe when I saw some moist eyes in almost every member of the South Team.

All because I had learnt before I turned.

Moral of the Story: Adaptability & adjustment is core to sales. One should not expect everyone in the team to adjust to you, you have got to adapt to the new environment. Only then you get accepted by the team & emerge as a true leader.

Delhi. June 2010

I had joined Mars Chocolates in June 2010 as one of the early Associates in the India Business with the designation as "Sales Operations Manager – Delhi NCR". Mars does not refer to people working for it as "Employees" but "Associates". A simple nomenclature change but alters the paradigm of engagement from Output-Salary Equation to Emoticnal Connection. Mars had a flourishing Pet Food brand 'Pedigree' which they had been able to build as category from scratch over the last five years. While initially when the Chocolate business was launched in India, it was done by the Pedigree network which soon failed as the Route to Market of both products is completely different & therefore it was decided that in order to drive efficiency, performance can't be compromised.

My first day at Mars was the induction in the Pedigree warehouse in Okhla Phase 1 New Delhi. I found the address with a lot of difficulty in the Non Google map days. The weather was merciless & so was the smell of the Pet Food as I entered the warehouse. For someone not used to the smell, it was an excruciating day as the smell filled my complete senses. Chocolates could not be stored here as it required a cold room to maintain temperatures which was managed by Snowman in Faridabad. After the initial brief during the day, I was packed off to Bangalore to understand the business in South as it was flourishing because of the high presence of Modern Trade & Supermarkets.

South Market has always been more developed from the Influence of the Middle East as well as High Disposable Income which has a direct rub off on the quality of the Trade or Shopping Experience for the consumer. Through the week I travelled the length & breadth of Bangalore city from Banashankari to Whitefield & Rajaji Nagar to Koramangala & picked up extremely useful learnings for executing in Delhi. While on the last day on the field, I got a call from my Line Manager (Vivek) informing & congratulating me as that I was being promoted as the Zonal Business Manager for North & East India albeit on a lighter note, there was no business or sales worth mentioning in this part of the Country.

I came back to Delhi after the Bangalore sojourn & got down to work. The basic building block to right Route to Market (RTM) was to build product reach to Hundreds of Mom & Pop Grocery Stores & for that to happen, we needed a distributor to fuel this transaction. However there was different challenge in building a distribution network for Mars Chocolates. Unlike Cadbury Dairy Milk which can sustain temperatures till 37-38 Degrees, Snickers, Mars, Galaxy, Twix & Bounty from Mars Chocolates India portfolio would start melting beyond 28 Degrees because of the high content of Cocoa Butter which gives it the real chocolaty flavour. Most of India mainly North India remains above 28 Degrees for most parts of the year, which meant the Distribution had to be a cold chain compliant distribution.

This would entail importing chocolates in cold containers from across the world to Mumbai Port, then transporting to various Warehouses across the country in cold vans, storage in warehouse in cold warehouses, shipping to distributors in cold vans, storage at distributor in cold rooms, sending the supplies to retailers in cold boxes & then storing in refrigerators at retailers. This was an uphill task considering the Chilling Infrastructure in the country in 2010 was quite poor with extended power cuts being a norm than an exception. This was a major distribution handicap along with the extreme focus on quality as a guiding principle of Mars.

Resultant, entire Delhi NCR had couple of distributors doing miniscule business. My first objective was to find a distributor but there was no one interested. I went from pillar to post meeting 50+ distributors but drew a blank. "What is the expected Business per Month", "What is the area you want me to cover", "How many Outlets", "How many manpower required for order booking & supplies"," What about Chocolate damages because of melting". I had very little for answer for. One such expedition led me in to the bylanes of Raja Garden in West Delhi. Some retailer gave reference of a person interested in distributor ship. I was jumping with excitement & called him up to be led upto to his place of business through directions via multiple calls on the mobile phone. After a frantic walk of 20 minutes, I reached his place to find out his business was fresh milk supplies. All I could find there were buffaloes & cows. I used all references to find distributors to the extent of taking bills from Retailers who got supplies from distributors of other brands and cold calling them. No one was keen to take up the distributorship of Mars Chocolates.

While we could manage the cold chain from Mumbai Port to the distributor, we needed right storage infrastructure at his point. This required the distributor to build a wooden enclosure with 1.5 Ton Split AC & running it for 18 hours to maintain 18 degrees temperature. Also, for the supplies we needed thick shipper boxes & chill pads used for transporting medicines & injections. The chill pads would be frozen in deep freezers. In the shipper boxes, the base layer & side walls would be of the frozen chill pads from the deep freezer, on which the chocolates boxes would be stacked which would then be covered up again by frozen chills pads. This would ensure chocolate quality being maintained. Most consumers in India buy chocolates from retailers & then put it inside the refrigerator. But when take out the chocolate out for consumption, a white layer is seen around the chocolate which is the fat which had burst out due to the temperature shock or the heat. All this infrastructure would cost 75,000. No wonder I was not able to convince any distributor to take up distribution for Mars Chocolates because no one was willing to make an upfront investment of 75,000 without any guarantee of sales & ROI.

I was thinking & trying very hard to make it work but to no avail. I started looking for people with no experience of distribution but had the money to finance this Route to Market. Finally after a lot of search, I found one called Shakuntala Traders to service an upcoming suburb of Ghaziabad (UP) called Indirapuram. He did not know ABC of distribution but I made him agree to just finance while entire operation would be run by our team. In order to run this, I hired three FOS (Feet on Street). I remember meeting him in a shanty in East Delhi from where he ran his catering business. I was shaky at the start but I knew that I had to do something to get the distribution off the blocks. Sometimes we wait too long for the perfect solution which never arrives.

We located a shop in Khora Village at Noida Ghaziabad border as the storage & supply point. We asked the financer to invest in the infrastructure i.e Wooden Enclosure, Split AC, Deep Freezer, Shipper Boxes & Chill Pads. The bait was the money invested will be returned back to him in 12 Monthly Claims. With the infrastructure done we placed the first order of 2 Lacs.

Next was the big challenge of supplies. Our FOS had been visiting market, booking the orders from Retailers but Shakuntala Traders did not supply those orders citing one flimsy reason after another.

One day I was sitting in the Pedigree Warehouse when I received a call from Lalit, our FOS that supplies for the day had been cancelled. We were losing face in front of Retailers as well as the team. I also knew that Shakuntala Traders had zero understanding or inclination of distribution, therefore me & my FOS, Lalit decided to do the distribution ourselves. We started market working in Indirapuram on a hot day in July & started opening outlets & taking orders. Very few interested retailers. Most said no citing the heat & season. "No demand, I don't know your brand, Come after 3 months in October, Price is high, I will see next time, No customer has asked for it." We received a volley of rejections. The day's count was 42 Calls 4 Productive 1200 Rupee Sales. It was disheartening.

After 8 Hours of real back breaking work, drenched in sweat, I did not know how to circumvent this challenge. Sometimes in life you get Eureka moments from unexpected people. While I was contemplating the next steps, I saw a Bicycle rider with boxes of Orbit & Boomer chewing Gum delivering to Retailers while taking orders. I could a faint light at the end of the tunnel.

Not to give up, I told my FOS to try a Ready Stock. Ready Stock is a hugely beneficial method where limited sku's are present. But the Retailer places the order & it is delivered on the spot, payment collected & transaction closed. This is mostly followed in Cigarette, Gums, Confectionery & Salty Snacks (Chips) product categories. I used to drive a Ford Ikon Diesel during those times. My Ford Ikon became the Ready Stock Unit. We got two shipper boxes with chill pads & 1 manual bill book & set out on the journey. The back seat of my car was loaded with large shipper boxes. I dodged the traffic cops stationed on the Noida Ghaziabad border to enter Indirapuram & begin our sojourn.

First call, productive. The thrill of selling 313 Rupee box of 24 pcs of 15 gm chocolate bar was unbelievable & memorable. Order delivered & cash collected. Second call, productive. We did 25 calls on the day & made it a beat. Beat is a Route or Area that one services in a pattern on a fixed frequency. It was so much easier to convince retailers to buy with a box of chilled Snickers in hand. All the queries & doubts raised previously, magically vanished. We covered 30 Outlets & 22 out of them placed Order. 10,000+ Rupee Sales. Lots of sweat but at the end of the day, the empty shipper boxes with 3000 Rupee Cash Sales made it a day to cherish.

As weeks rolled by, this beat of 30 outlets branched out to 3 routes of 35 outlets each with the distribution muscle matching cadburys in that suburb. All of it was possible because we did not give up on the idea & made it work come what may.

Moral of the Story – Tenacity is the core value to drive sales.

Learning 1

Bangalore. May 2015

I had been living in the weather paradise of India called then 'Bangalore' for two years. Somehow I never got used to calling the city as Bengaluru. The old name had a charm to it. Incidentally while living in Bangalore, I was also supposed to sell Nivea products i.e Deodorants, Body Lotions, Cremes, Lip Balms, Shower Gels to the consumers of four Indian states of Kerala. Karnataka, Tamil Nadu & Andhra Pradesh.

I had already spent ten years in the trade by then & was getting bored with the monotonous routine of running after Secondary Sales for first twenty days in a month & Primary Sales for the balance ten days in the month. For the uninitiated, Secondary Sales refers to the sales that the distributor does on brand's behalf to the retailer, while primary sales is the sales of products from the company to the distributor. Irrespective of the brand & regardless of the location, this is a constant in every FMCG (Fast Moving Consumer Goods) Salesman's life.

I had a taken up a mini office with one cubicle, ten workstations & two conference rooms in the leafy suburb of Koramangala on a sharing basis or co-working which was unheard of in those days. While the entire team remained on the field, I was the sole occupant of the Office, which naturally meant that I would doze off in my chair for couple of times in the day. My eyes had just started to droop after I finished my lunch but was woken up by my signature ring tone of my Nokia mobile phone. "Hi, I'm Vinayak from New Era Consultants". I knew a consultant was calling me to offer the same run-down Regional Manager role in some company which meant the same boring routine, I answered the call casually. "Yes Vinayak, tell me. I'm looking for a new opportunity but not in FMCG".

"Well we have something for you in retail, fashion retail". It got me interested & I was eager to hear more. My excitement was increasing only to get deflated immediately with Vinayak's next sentence. "The opening is in Kolkata with Pantaloons". "Kolkata. No way," I mean who goes to Kolkata from Bangalore. "Sorry Vinayak, I will let this pass". The opportunity was appealing & the location was repelling. I was not able to get rid of this thought on the drive back to home from office. I was sceptical of my wife's reaction to Kolkata as I could visualize a vehement & vigorous shaking of her head. But this was something which was different to what I was doing or had ever done in my career. While I was deliberating in my head, I decided to look up who was heading the business of Pantaloons. My LinkedIn popped up the name "Paras".

I was taken aback as Paras was heading the Human Resource Function for Pantaloons & he was incidentally the guy who recruited me from campus ten years ago as the Management Trainee & saw my progress in the

Aditya Birla Group for first two years of my career. "I will drop in a text on LinkedIn & let's see what happens", I thought. "Hi Priyaranjan, I remember you. How have you been". My message was answered by Paras in a couple of hours. I spoke to him & then underwent three interview rounds, post which I was offered the position of Zonal Business Head East Zone Pantaloons.

It was extremely difficult to convince my wife to relocate to Kolkata. She relented on one condition that we would visit the city & finalise our place of stay. Her decision to relocate would depend on where we would live. I complied dutifully & gingerly got ready for the relocation. I was myself unsure of what to expect in an alien city with no friends or family with a new job in an entirely new sector which I hardly knew apart from a consumer.

We landed in Kolkata in the extremely humid month of May on a mission to find a school for my son & a place to live. It was also my secret trip to the city to see & experience Pantaloons stores & boost my self-confidence to drive a completely new type of work vehicle.

After fixing up the school admissions for my son in New Town School which was located in the outskirts of city near the Airport, my next objective was to finalise a place to stay which was a prerequisite for my wife's decision to relocate to Kolkata. I went about looking at few places in New Town before freezing a condominium called Rosedale Gardens. It was a sight to behold. New construction with 25% occupancy, spic & span, brand new unused semi furnished apartment on the 15th Floor with a beautiful view of Kolkata city. In fact, I could see the flood light towers of the Iconic Eden Gardens from one of the bedrooms. The icing on the cake was the size of 2800 Sq. Ft with four bedrooms at the monthly rent of 38,000. People living in Mumbai, Gurgaon & Bangalore would jump from the same 15th Floor if such an offer was given to them. My wife & son were overjoyed with the choice & thus the decision to move to Kolkata was done & dusted.

I had visited a couple of Pantaloons stores in Bangalore in the past week therefore had an idea of what to expect. Also from my previous visits to Kolkata I knew that South City Mall was the biggest shopping mall in Kolkata. Armed with my consumer understanding of Pantaloons stores in Bangalore & knowledge about South City Mall, I entered the Pantaloons store. This place was different from the stores in Bangalore as chalk is to cheese. The iconic Pantaloons store in South City was spread over two levels with each level of 30,000 Sq Ft of never ending assortment & display of fashion. I was spell bound & confused by the enormity of the store & also jittery about what I had signed up for. Many months later, I saw another Pantaloons store in Kolkata which was larger in size than South City which was Kankurgachi. Coming back to my experience on the day, I was not able to freeze the starting point of understanding the business since this was unknown territory & a new game for me to play.

I had figured in life that the best way to learn anything new was to get the pearls of wisdom not from the top but from the front lines. In my regular visits to new towns & cities, I would always chat with the cab driver to understand the pulse of the place, famous spots to eat authentic cuisine & the political, law & order ecosystem. The kind of in depth knowledge that these cab drivers have would put the city encyclopedia to shame. I tried the same trick to learn about the business from the font line salesmen. The same salesmen/women whom all of us encounter in our daily lives whenever we go out to shop for anything from grocery to fruits, vegetables to fashion, lifestyle, consumer electronics & even cars. Similar to cab drivers, these front liners have tremendous knowledge of the ground situation because they are closest to the consumer. If ever one wants to get smarter in business, they should interact with 5 consumers daily. After a month, it is 100% guaranteed that you would have become sharper & crisper with the needs & requirements of the business.

I made friends with couple of these Front Liners called Fashion Associates in the store & took them to be my Guru's. "Hi, my name is Ranjan & I need your help. I'm joining as a Store Manager for Max in Bhubaneswar but I don't have any retail experience. I'm trying to learn this business by speaking to Sales Associates like you in order to bolster my fundamentals of the industry, would you please help". I spoke for 30 seconds in one breath thereby forcing Subhash & Mithun (Sales Associates) to accede to my request.

Lesson 1 – "How strong are your knees & ankles" asked one of them. I was surprised. "Sir, because these bones are the first casualty in Retail. If you have not worked in retail & don't have strong bones, your body weight will put such pressure on your joints which you will not be able to take after three days". I got the message because if one holds a glass for a minute, nothing happens. If you hold it for 5 minute, nothing happens. If you hold it for 10 minutes, hands starts aching. But if you hold for 2 hours, the arms will give away. The Job requires 8-9 Hours of standing putting the entire body weight on knee & ankle joints with the added pressure of servicing the customer with a smile, even if the body is cracking up & top it with some disappointment of missed sales & icing of verbal abuse. I mumbled "I will exercise & make them strong". It set me thinking for a while on the choice I was making. This definitely required not only strong bones but thick skin as well.

Lesson 2 – "Sir, I can predict with 90% accuracy who is window shopper & who is a serious shopper" said one of them. I asked them "How". "We spend 10 hours serving 50-60 customers every day. We can tell who will buy, how much they are going to buy just by observing their body language & their eyes. The way they touch & feel the garment gives us an indication if the product is in their affordability range or not. However, if we can hold them for 15 minutes & make them try one or two garments, then the chances of sales conversion become more than 90%. Therefore, Sir, the key is to hold their interest & attention for 15 minutes. I try very hard to cross that critical time cliff".

I was spell bound by the logical, analytical & observational ability of these guys. "Wow. We talk of training these guys in classroom sessions. It should be the reverse, they should train the Management". There is ZERO substitute to spending time on the floor listening & observing the Customers in action. No Book, no theory can teach you as much.

Lesson 3 – "What is the reason for customers to keep coming back this store to shop again & again considering there are options available in Online & Offline now ," I asked. "Sir, there is no alternative to a good product. Product is the hero of the store & the primary reason for customer to come back. Secondary reason is the service which includes understanding the customer requirements, staff behaviour, fitting room experience, basic hygiene in the store & lastly the ease & speed of check out. Rest everything else is for internal company folks. Customer is not bothered." I was astounded by the level of understanding of the Customer Service requirements which resided in these Fashion Sales Associates. They were referring to the basic requirements of the consumer which most times brands forget to fulfil & settle for higher order thinking

I got my trip's worth. My learning in retail had started thanks to my front line Guru's which continues till date.

Moral of the story: Today's Consumer has changed. They are looking for relatable people, connected stories & shopping sufficiency. No wonder all the recent Bollywood blockbusters are the One's narrating lives of Common Men & Women in hinterland India. Gone out of the picture are the Swiss Alps & replaced by Mirzapur's & Ballia's.

Risk!

Kolkata. June 2015

The alarm clock beeped at 5.30 am on an overcast June morning. Lazily, I got up from the bed looking into the beautiful blueish hues of Kolkata skyline. It was my supposed to be my first day in the Zonal Office of Pantaloons located at the iconic Camac Street in Kolkata. It was little unusual for me to see such daylight in the early morning. "Sun rises in the East", I remembered the lesson learnt in Class V.

I had a very light breakfast & rushed down from my 15th Floor apartment in Rosedale Gardens in New Town area looking for an Uber ride to Camac Street. "430" was the fare flashed on my app. I hastily booked as I wanted to be in office at sharp 9.30 am. The 20 km drive took 35 minutes which was a breeze coming from the city of Bangalore where a 5km drive would take the same time. As the cab drove through the expansive roads, I noticed excessive usage of blue & white colour on the Metro pillars, houses, buildings all reinforcing the fact that I was in the land of Maa, Maati, Maanush. There was a rustic charm about the city with the unfinished & dilapidated Metro pillars on one side and the majestic

ITC Sonar Bangla on the other side of MAA flyover. I crossed the famous Seven-point traffic signal which is extremely exciting for someone seeing it for the first time.

The traffic system in central Kolkata can be extremely confusing for a new towner as most streets are one way & the traffic flow changes direction from morning to evening. So, if Camac Street traffic flows North to South in the morning, it changes to South to North in the evening & it is managed by the best dressed cops in India riding their red bullet motorcycles in their strapping boots, white uniforms & Airforce like Aviators.

It took me 10 minutes to find the entrance to 22, Camac Street 2nd floor which resembled like a maze on the first visit. Aditya Birla Fashion & Retail logo with Pantaloons emblazoned shone brightly on a newly minted steel A4 plate. I was greeted with a wide eyed gentleman "Subroto" wearing a crisp, clean uniform. "Apani kara saathe dekha karata cana" in chaste Bengali asked Subroto which meant, whom do you want to meet ?. "I understood half Bengali as I spent two years of my childhood in Guwahati, Assam where I picked up the Assamese language. I shrugged my shoulders & gave him a smile & walked in. The clock showed 9.35 am & the office was deserted. Worn out desks, run down furniture, hanging tube lights, incoherent colour combinations, damp walls greeted me.

I was deep in my thoughts, when a young boy wished me "Good Morning Sir". "Hey, is it a holiday today," I asked. "No, Sir". "Then how come no one is here" I asked. I was just about to finish my last word when the hymn of Aditya Birla Group called the Aditya Vandana started playing in the Office. "Sir, people will come in by 11 am". I got little more in depth understanding on how lunch breaks would extend into Carrom board sessions leading to Tea breaks & then sunset beckons at 5pm.

"We are getting rogered in East, which is our strongest market". These words from the CEO & the Business Director at my induction in Mumbai made more sense to me now. "We have opened only two stores of Pantaloons in last three years in our strongest market. I want you to do something about it." Said Sumit, the then CEO of Pantaloons. I had to change the situation pretty fast. The first thing I did was to throw away the carrom board & uprooted the long wire connecting the lamp over the carrom. Then I would reach office by 9.30 am & stand in the alley ushering in the people to their seats. Suddenly, mornings became rushed for a lot of people & office became quieter. I had ruffled a lot of feathers really hard.

Today's day & age, you cannot expect consumers to come to you. You have to reach out to them. Pantaloons in East was stuck in a time warp. The previous brand owners i.e Future Group knew the pulse of Kolkata so were able to establish & run an extremely profitable business because of low real estate price & manpower costs coupled with low competition. The current management knew very little of Kolkata & East with many of them had not travelled beyond Kolkata, so they were dependent on one person, Suresh who claimed to know East market like the back of his hand. The management was extremely dependent on this person to the extent that they did not realise that he had become a big liability than an asset. He knew the East so much so that only two new stores of Pantaloons could be opened in entire East in three years.

It had been a Month when I had taken over as Business Head & I was getting fidgety because every time I would send a proposal, it would be shot down over illogical revertals on loss of brand reputation, future risk of good locations & myriad of reasons. However every cloud has a silver lining. After a long gap there was a new store opening of Pantaloons in South Kolkata on Sharath Chandra Bose Road which was a stone's throw away from one of the iconic Pantaloons stores in Camac Street. I had no role to play in this as this was signed, designed, executed, readied by my predecessor & Suresh. One day I decided to visit the store & booked an Uber ride. Before I could answer few of my whats app messages, I had arrived at the destination. I was confused as to why we had selected to open a three Level 10,000 Sq Ft Store at 200/- Per Square Foot which was 1 Kms away from 25,000 Sq Ft Flagship Store & Landmark of our Brand in Kolkata.

The rent was exorbitantly high at 20 Lacs per month. Though I had spent very little time in retail, I knew the maths & common sense was not stacking up. Why would a consumer come to a place which has 60% lesser choice thereby leading to very low footfall translating to low sales resulting in a major operating loss. The store opened like the Aamir Khan starrer Laal Singh Chadha which promised so much but doomed at the box office, the new store collapsed in sales on day 1 of the opening. My initial assessment turned out to be correct & the Store bombed big time so much so it shook the confidence of the management in opening new stores in Kolkata. Pantaloons store failing in Kolkata was akin to Aamir Khan starrer not being able to fill the cinemas seats. It was unthinkable but the reality was that the brand had taken the consumer for a guaranteed purchaser from wherever & what so ever format it opened.

While I could not be blamed for the disaster but it shook me to the core & obstructed my decision making as fear of failure ran amok through my head. Mistakes in physical retail are very costly & loosely mimic an estranged marriage. Cleaning up the mess is hugely cumbersome with unimaginable write offs. But I had to push the needle. I was recruited for exactly the same purpose. I did not want to get out while defending & not scoring runs. I wanted to try & hit the ball hard to take the team to victory even if that meant, I could get out. I started scouting for opportunities with my team. I had spent enough time travelling in cabs in Kolkata to understand that like Mumbai, the lifeline of Kolkata is the suburban railway network. People travelled from Upcountry to Shop in the famous Burra Bazaar & New Market areas. This provided a massive opportunity to expand outside the main city I shortlisted stations which had the maximum crowd within a radius of 30 km from Central Kolkata.

First probable location came in Baruipur which is 25 Kms from City Centre in South 24 Parganas. I distinctly remember the late afternoon on a Friday of the 4th week of July of 2015. I was sitting in my cubicle when my phone buzzed. "Sir, I have got a running store in

Baruipur, which is 10,000 Sq ft. We can visit next week & see". The call was from Ritin, one of two resources in charge of leading expansion of stores in East India. I jumped out of my seat & said, "Let's go now". I booked a cab & within one hour I was standing in front of shut down City Life Store. The store sold apparel & general merchandise in the mass pricing segment of less than 500 rupees.

I spent one hour looking up the entire store, all the floors, its façade, traffic flow, closest market, nearby railway station, place to park two wheelers, customer dressing sense & then arrived at the decision to go ahead. Since a lot of work which is required in a retail store of flooring, ceiling, air conditioning was already completed, it meant lower capital expenditure & if things would go well, faster payback. We negotiated on the rent & closed the deal then & there at 50 Rupees per Square Ft.

On way drive back home which took me two hours, I kept rehearsing as to how I would pitch this store to the CEO because I knew if I followed the protocol of going through Suresh & the National Operations Head, it would lead to a dead end. If I would bypass them it would mean, insubordination & burning permanent bridges which was not a good option considering I had just joined the business & they were old hands. I was scared because it could lead to creation of circumstances which could lead to my ouster. I was confused, anxious & perplexed with the two options at hand. I decided to risk it to fix it. Someone had to bite the bullet for the sake of business growth in East, so if I was the chosen one, I should not be backing out.

I wrote the proposal email directly to the CEO breaking protocol & keeping both the gentlemen in cc. As expected, Sumit was super excited & pumped while others were raging. "It is a disastrous call which will destroy the brand permanently in East, we should not do it" quick reply came from Suresh on my proposal. I was headlong into the fight. I could not pull back now. I called up Sumit & told him clearly if they had recruited me to change things then he would need to believe me & support my decision. I put my neck on the line & put my hand accepting responsibility in case it did not work. "Ok go ahead", the email said from Sumit.

It was show time now. I had to make it successful for the direction of the future stores to be opened became clearer. One thing which never deserted me was keeping Consumer at Centre. So, I decided to keep Exit Price Point at 999. The look & feel of the store was intentionally kept subdued to ensure that the consumer in that LIG catchment felt welcome & not intimidated. Men's Fashion was given Lion's Share & kept on Ground Floor as RMG (Ready Made Garments) in small town India is still Men's dominated. Women Western Wear was miniscule because here Indian Women folk still prefer Sarees & Ready to Stitch Fabric. Kids Fashion was positioned as trump card.

Next step was to create Buzz in Catchment. I decided to use Auto Backs, Cloth Banners all shouting "Fatafati Daam Fatafati Fashion 99 – 999" Fatafati is an endearing Bengali word for Fantastic. Then the Masterstroke. I got three Leading Ladies Momani, Mohua & Nandini from Zee Bangla & Star Jalsa channels for the Store Opening. They were the popular daily soaps queen on television. And to ensure I left nothing to chance I put up 2 Full Stack Tables of Kids T Shirt which was Old Season Merchandise at Flat 99.

I waited with bated breath as the D- Day arrived. My blood pressure starting increasing with each passing hour. "Sir till now very low footfall" informed the store manager. I was sweating but somewhere God's were testing my patience & smiling as the crowd started to build up from 2pm. By 3.30 Pm the Two Tables of Kids T Shirts at Flat 99 had become empty. There was long queue at the billing counter. I stood outside observing the consumer reactions as they stepped out of store. Most were extremely happy with their purchase. It became chaotic at 5 Pm. We had to call the cops to restrict Customer Entry. The Store was on fire. 7 Lacs on Day 1

I knew we were on the path to profitability & the way to opening many more such stores in East.

Moral of the Story: if you don't risk disliking in the organization, you will never fix the problem.

Acceptability!

Mumbai. June 2013

"Ladies & Gentlemen. We are about to start our descent into Chennai. We are currently 200 kms away from Chennai & expect to land in 30 mins. Cabin crew please prepare for arrival". I was woken up from deep sleep by this sharp announcement on a sunny June morning of 2013. I had taken an early morning flight from Mumbai to Chennai with my supervisor Dev. I had joined Nivea as the Regional Manager South & therefore as a part of induction & introduction Dev was taking me to Chennai, Hyderabad & Bangalore to meet the Area Managers.

There was a time gap between my predecessor leaving & my joining which was filled in by Dev directly during this period. I had spent four years of my youth in Bangalore studying Instrumentation Technology which I hardly understood or remembered anything after I wrote my final exams but living & working in South India was different. I was up for the challenge mentally.

The flight landed & as we walked out of the airport, I noticed a smiling face with a thin twirling moustache wearing a white shirt with Nivea emblazoned on the chest waking towards us. "Hello, Sir, how was the flight?" asked Chandan in his trademark jovial style. I shook hands with him & exchanged pleasantries. Weather in Chennai & understanding of Hindi is a fantastic conversation starter. Chandan was as uncomfortable in Hindi as I was in Chennai weather because I could feel the sweat dripping from my back due to the trapped heat of the inner vest which I was wearing to protect myself from the chilly temperatures of the Airport & Aircraft.

Dev joked with Chandan about something related to food leading to a full-scale laughter from all of us. I noticed something peculiar with Chandan that he never shook his head up down or left right, it was always in circles. While he did so on habit, it confused the other person on his acceptance or denial of the situation. We stopped at the iconic Saravana Stores in T Nagar to check up on Nivea stocks & offtakes. Dev in his inimitable style put his reading glass on his head to check the product up & close. I stood silently observing the body language of Chandan & his Sales Officer. We visited couple of more stores before landing at Murugan Idly for the lunch. "Sir, what will you have?" Chandan asked me very politely. "Two Meals & One Idly" ordered Chandan. My first impressions of Chandan was very positive as he came across as courteous, polite, compliant, sharp, cheerful & confident. He knew his craft really well.

We finished the market visit & headed to our hotel. While both of us checked in, Chandan waited for us at the lobby area for dinner. I quickly put my overnighter in the room & came down to spend time with him. "Who all are there in your family?" I asked. He explained his family tree, his experience, his life, his challenges. It seemed like he was waiting to uncork. I listened to him very patiently absorbing all his comments, ideas, struggles & suggestions. I knew I had touched a chord with him because he spoke for 20 minutes non-stop while I just smiled. "Sir, what about you, Family? Kids?". I gave him a brief peek into my personal life & past experiences. I picked up something very important from the conversation with him. The best way to a teammates or colleagues heart is by remembering their kids names. It makes a world of difference to the other person as you come across as genuine & caring.

We wrapped up dinner quickly as we had an early morning flight to Hyderabad. We landed in the city of Nizams to be welcomed by Jagan at the Airport. Jagan spoke Hindi but in the typical Hyderabadi style. He looked very young for his age which I complimented him for. He had a broad smile on his face because I had reduced his age by 5 years in my approximation of his experience. He was not as talkative & expressive as Chandan responding to only questions with his mono syllable answers. We stopped at a store called Beauty Centre at Banjara Hills. We were greeted by a charming Nivea Beauty Advisor dressed in Nivea Blue dress. "How is sales, how are your numbers against target, what about the new deodorant response? Dev fired a volley of questions towards the beauty advisor. She could just mumble up a coherent sentence which meant that the sales was very challenging because of aggressive promotions in modern Trade stores & consumers gravitating towards those stores. Another volley of questions from Dev followed to which I nudged Jagan to answer as I could sense the discomfort in the

Beauty Advisor's body language. Jagan spoke in a very soft & feeble tone stating that More Hyper & D Mart were running a very high consumer promotion thus impacting sales in the general trade channel.

We visited couple of more stores before settling into a hearty meal of Biryani at the famous Paradise Biryani. While I ordered a vegetable Biryani, Dev & Jagan had bowlful of Gosht & Chicken biryani. I noticed Jagan had a penchant for spicy food. While it may seem to be an innocuous observation, it is always important to understand the food preferences of the people working with you. Jagan took us to meet the biggest distributor of Hyderabad by the name Sai Srinivasa Agencies. "How is the business Sir". Dev asked. "Modern Trade is giving such consumer offers that it is below our landing price or the price at which company is billing to us. How can sales grow Sir"? Dev was stumped with the response & brushed it by asking for proof, explaining it could be one off, basically trying to wrap the issue and throw it in the bin.

We packed up from the city to head to the airport for our next destination which was the silicon valley of India & arguably the most vibrant & happening city in India. "You have landed at Kempegowda International Airport, Bengaluru. Have a pleasant stay," said the air hostess in a boring SOP like tone. We got out of the airport to be greeted with the most famous thing about Bangalore, which was the weather. The cool gush of air suddenly threw a chill around the body. It seemed like a Delhi November & different world to the hot Hyderabad & humid Chennai. It was late in the evening so we checked into hotel to stay overnight. Since Dev was flying out in the evening to Mumbai & the airport in

Bangalore is not in Bangalore but nearer to Hyderabad meant that we had to start the day early.

I had a quick breakfast & came down so the lobby to locate Suresh, our Area Manager in Bangalore. Suresh could easily be spotted from a distance. He looked visibly edgy & sported a peck of Sandalwood on his forehead. He seemed to the typical good Kannadiga man who visited temples, worked hard & went straight home, someone who would not relate directly to be in sales function. I walked up to him, "Hi Suresh". "Hello, Sir, how are you?" said Suresh in a sharp rustic English. His mannerisms & his accent clearly gave out his vast experience & his journey of a ranker from a frontline distributor salesman to an Area Manager. I always have had a soft corner for people who fight the system & still grow under the weight of gravity of pedigree, fancy degrees & fluid communication.

Suresh quickly went through his bio with me to be cut short by me asking him about his family. "Sir, I have two daughters, one is in class eight & other one is special child. She needs physiotherapy everyday & needs her mother for her normal routine". I listened in rapt attention to the struggles which people have & still came to work fighting & smiling. I put my arm around him & gave him the confidence that he was a fighter & that we shall together turn around the business. I asked him about the work challenges & what was impacting growth of Nivea in Bangalore considering the purchasing power of consumers, brand awareness & the supermarket nature of retail trade in the city. "Shaab" it was mix of Sir & Sahab that Suresh would say, "Peoples are working properly, distributors working properly, problem is credit outstanding in market. Distributors don't want to extend more credit in market & Supermarkets don't pay. So, we are not able to do right primary, Shaab".

As I was going on trying to understand the situation, Dev came in the discussion & we started for the market. We covered the first outlet in Commercial Street, the famous hub for fashion & lifestyle in Bangalore. Displays were nice arranged & Suresh had turned the store Nivea blue. It looked like the retailer was working as Nivea franchisee. I still can't fathom why are field staff scared in showing market reality to the management & why is the management so naïve in believing that this is for real. I told Suresh taking him aside "Please don't show this dream to me in the future. I want to see & understand the ground reality because only then I will be able to find some solution, because if everything is perfect, why is sales not growing?". Suresh smiled back & in his energetic tone replied "Yes, Shaab". We covered some more outlets after which Dev left for the airport & started my relocation process from Delhi to Bangalore.

It is extremely critical to earn respect from one's teams if one wants to emerge as a leader & not a boss. Through my first couple of visits & meeting with my direct reports, I was trying to endear myself to them, earn respect, lend an ear to their real problems. A lot of times, people get shouted upon when they share the situation & reality which makes the other person lose respect for the leader.

Moral of the Story: The first step to leading a team is to get accepted by the team.

Responsibility!

Kolkata. June 2015

"What is Sharodiya Saaj Utsav?", I whispered into Souvik's ear. "It is our name to the promotions during Durga Pooja", he whispered back. I was sitting in a dilapidated room which jokingly could be called a conference room in Zonal Office of Pantaloons, a part of Aditya Birla Fashion & Retail at 22, Camac Street Kolkata. I was taking over as the Zonal Business Head for East at Pantaloons, a pioneer in the world of organized fashion retail. It was minor detail that I had no clue about Retail coming from ten years of hardcore Sales & Distribution experience in Fast Moving Consumer Goods.

The entire Management Team along with Marketing & Visual Merchandising team had flown to Kolkata to discuss & finalize the Pujo (Durga Pooja) plan. Pujo was the jugular vein of the profitability for East Zone of Pantaloons & the main artery of EBITDA for the company. I was not able to understand the hype & hoopla around it till I was explained its significance by a native Kolkatan. He said all festivals in India are one day or two day affairs be it Diwali, Holi, Chatth,

Onam, Dusshehra, Christmas, Eid. But Pujo was different because all Bengalis wherever they would be in the whole world would descend into their native towns with maximum of them making beeline for Kolkata with their families. The festival is such that it starts from Panchomi (fifth day of Navratas), Shosti, Soptami, Ashtomi, Naomi. It is a five-day festival where three pairs of new clothes are needed every day which means fifteen new pairs for all family members, thus making it the biggest shopping & gifting event in the whole world.

The enormity of the festival is such that all brands of any significance in the country starting from face care, hair care, perfumes, consumer electronics, jewellery, even steel bars, cement, paints would jostle for smallest of spaces for advertising on the roads, pandals, newspapers, stations, airports & shopping malls. I did not realise the full impact of the festival till I experienced it first-hand. Newspapers delivery stops, Milk packets run out, Bread is not manufactured. The morning & afternoons seems like the Covid induced lockdows in the city while the evenings & nights magically transform into the shack parties on Goan beaches. Family, friends, acquaintances indulge fully in their "adda" sessions & "pandal hopping" running into wee hours of the morning then sleeping the day off to repeating the cycle for five days. It is a sight to behold which one feels horribly out of place the first year & then Pujo spirit takes over in the next year. Somehow even for someone who did not have too many friends or any relatives in Kolkata, Pujo became my favourite part of the year till the time I stayed in Kolkata. The city makes you fall in love with it slowly making you adjust with its slow heartbeat & laidback lifestyle so much so that I still miss

Kolkata though I have lived in Mumbai, Gurgaon, Noida, Bangalore.

The boardroom discussion was intense as the CEO kept on asking pointed questions expecting detailed responses from Souvik who seemed like KL Rahul facing a bullet deliveries from Shaheen Shah Afridi. Souvik was heading the business in East as the business Manager but was making the management sitting in Mumbai nervy about the business & market share loss in East which was the stranglehold of Pantaloons. I was tasked to take over from him & he was supposed to report to me. Entire team in East was divided into two with half of them with Souvik & the other half with Ananda who was a peer to Souvik but had lost out to him in the run for the leadership position. While both of them were civil to each other in public, they left no opportunity in tearing apart each other in private. Ananda was also the go to man for the CEO in East & had a hotline with him. When I was explained this dynamic, I just smiled to myself thinking "Muskuraiye, aap Kalkatta mein hain" because I did not know ABC of retail plus I was supposed to topple the main man in the region who did not gel with half the team & I had absolutely zero understanding of layout, location, processes, product.

Time flew in the next few months & we were on the doorstep of Durga Pooja forty-five day period. We were running a done to death promotion of bedsheets & Duffle Bags. "How many bedsheets & bags will I take?" was the constant refrain from the customers. I spent hours on the shopping floor observing & understanding consumer behaviour. As expected, we had a below average Durga Pooja sales but I had got my cues for the next year.

The beauty of retail is that one never gets bored. It's like a never-ending saga which throws up surprises every day. Festivals lead to season changes to English Calendar New Year to Republic-day to Valentine's day to Holi to Indian Calendar New Year to regional festivals to Ramzan interspersed with End of Season Sales twice a year. Since it's a jam-packed calendar I did not realise that I was sitting in the month of June next year initiating the planning for Pujo. "Subhankar, I want to change this Sharodiya Saaj Utsav. This looks like we are celebrating the festival in 1970s. I need a punchy emotional & pulsating theme for Pujo this year". Subhankar was the Marketing lead for East. Pat came the reply from him. Sometimes in life you get a eureka moment or it is said in our religious conversations that Goddess Saraswati, power of knowledge & intelligence sits on your tongue very seldom. This was one of those moments. Subhankar said "Pujo Maane Pantaloons". I had never heard a better three-word punchier line than this which encompassed everything that we want to do for the consumers to come to shop to Pantaloons.

The pillars of the foundation were cast but it was in reality it meant only 1% job done. I asked my Executive Assistant to pull out the data of frequency of visits of shoppers for last 2 years to Pantaloons stores. The data reaffirmed my hunch that nearly 70% of shoppers had visited more than two times to shop during the Pujo period. It made sense because the quantum of self use & gifting is so high that purchases of garments happens in phases starting with Kids purchases, then ladies &

finally leading to Men's. I sensed a great opportunity to get the customer hooked to our format & increase their wallet share with us. I cut through all red tape & called up the CEO. "I will run a passport program this Pujo". "What is a passport promotion. I don't want you to take a risk on Pujo business. It will screw us till cows come home", blurted the CEO. I reassured him that I was taking a very sensible & calculated risk which could catapult our growths to 20% +.

My thought process was clear. I wanted to give the customer chance to choose their own gift this Pujo. There would be gifts at threshold purchase value of 4999,9999,16999 & 24,999. The gifts were planned to be Portico Double Bedsheets, 20 Pieces Borosil Dinner Set, VIP Trolley bag & 21" Samsung LED TV respectively. The added benefit was that the customer could club their purchases during the forty-five day period & choose the gift of their liking. The biggest advantage was that the customer did not have to take a bedsheet three times if they shopped for three time for 5000 each. They could club it & take a VIP trolley bag. While the thought was simple but to administer this glitch free for over 3 Lac customers, maintaining their purchase history, redemption data was going to be a herculean task.

Anyone who heard the concept, baulked at the idea. Naysayers, said it would fall flat & went to the CEO to scrap this experiment as it had the potential to degenerate into a disastrous EBITDA loss for the company & loss of face for the brand 'Pantaloons' in front of the customers. The CEO panicked & called me frantically but I was adamant. I knew in my heart & mind I was doing the right thing for the consumer. I told him clearly it is my idea & if it fails, I will take full responsibility for its failure & then it was the management's call to decide my future in the organization. Seldom had anyone shown such guts & gumption in front of the CEO & that too someone who was only one year old in the organization & was coming from a different industry.

"Hello, Mandeep, can you help me?" I sent a Whatsapp. I got a call back within a minute. Mandeep was the IT Head of the business & he was the most critical person because the backbone of the system hinged on the product development & glitch free execution. The current loyalty program did not have the capability to reset the customer sales to zero post redemption during the promotion nor did it recognize the start date & end date. Therefore, a new software had to be designed which could fetch the customer information & purchases during the promotion period, keep track of it & send reminders to shop xyz amount to reach the next gift milestone & once redeemed, reset the customer counter to zero & all this while talk to the existing loyalty program & our point of sale system. It seemed easy to do but someone had to write a code, create scenarios, anticipate bugs & plan debugging.

It was a mammoth ask to design & execute this in 60 days. But Mandeep agreed to take up the challenge & committed to deliver a bug free software. The other challenge was marketing first internally to our floor staffs & store managers & then to the external customers. I called a meeting of all store managers of Pantaloons East & split them into groups to ideate a breakthrough idea for Pujo. They were split into five working groups to brainstorms ideas for one day. I kept a close watch on their discussions & germinated the passport idea within two groups. They built a fabulous action plan around it & presented to the larger audience to a rousing & thundering applause. I had successfully overcome the first challenge. I knew if the idea came from amongst the team, it would have greater & quicker acceptability compared to the monologue delivered by me. With the internal customers buying into the plan, I began to give the final touch to the grand plan which was to reach the customers directly. It was an audacious idea to go to top 500 customers home & invite them to Pantaloons stores with a gift.

Everyone in the team was reluctant to execute this but I was relentless. I initiated this by visiting customers personally. I particularly remember visiting a neighbourhood in Behala, where the legendary Sourav Ganguly lives. The lady of the house was taken aback on seeing us & ask some pointed questions before allowing us in to her house. She could not believe that we had travelled 20 kms & spent one hour searching for her house to invite her to visit Pantaloons stores for Pujo shopping. She served us delicious Mishti (sweets) & hot cup of tea & promised to shop at Pantaloons. Soon we had hundreds of such stories where customers showered immense love & patronage to our plan.

The moment of truth finally arrived in the first week of September. I waited with bated breath to gauge the customer response. We had made elaborate trouble shooting plan in case customers would not receive sms for OTP or any other technical issue which they would face. The build-up was slow as the staff initially struggled to explain the program clearly. I reacted immediately by getting cue cards printed which explained the shopping journey & promotion plan. I was jittery & I felt the load of the entire world on my back as I had fought the system & taken a huge gamble in changing the status quo. I decided to get the customer feedback first hand by visiting Pantaloons stores on the first weekend. Customers were warming up to the plan which started to show great traction. The first weekend was the bigger than the best weekend of last year. I knew we were up to something special.

Team was buoyed by the positive reaction of the customers & the competition was stunned to see what we were pulling off. "Ab ki baar dhai sau paar" I had taken this slogan from the 2014 general election campaign of the Prime Minister, it was turning out to be true. That year was the biggest & bestest year in the history of Pantaloons. The name of the promotion "Passport Program" which I coined without any logic became the most spoken word in the entire organization. The legacy lives on with the Passport program, which continued to gives super success & cemented "Pujo Maane Pantaloons"

Moral of the Story: Responsibility for results by putting one's neck on the block is the only way to deliver path breaking results.

Engagement!

Greater Noida. May 2012

Orange alert was sounded off in the city of Delhi. There were advisories given out by Doctors to stay hydrated and avoid venturing out in the afternoons. North India was on literal fire with the hot blustery winds as temperatures were breaking all previous records. As is always the case, some pray for rain, some pray for summers, some pray for winters, I would always love the North Indian climate from October to February because the weather would be ideal to sell chocolates keeping it out in open displays at all Mom & Pop stores. I was responsible for the Sales & Distribution for one of the biggest global confectionary giant, Mars.

This summer was extra cruel as it was punctuated by long power disruptions thus crippling chillers & freezers. Mars Chocolates business in India was in its infancy in 2010. We had just begun to make some inroads through a trickle presence in the vast Mom & Pop retail landscape across the length & breadth of India. While we used to scale up our presence during the winter season as Mars Inc brands of chocolates Mars, Snickers, Galaxy, Bounty & Twix could sustain the ambient temperature, we had pull out of retail stores in the summers as chocolates would start melting & become liquid. This was different from other brands available in the market like Cadbury's or Nestle as Mars brands contained much higher percentage of cocoa butter giving it the smoother taste but resulting in melting at temperatures beyond 28 degrees. Therefore, summers were a tightrope walk in order to maintain quality of the product & the sales distribution of the product.

We would always bank much more on the Modern Trade outlets in the summer months as they had much better infrastructure of air conditioning & chillers. We would scramble for dairy chiller units through plastic fixtures which could hang on its walls to ensure product stability. I had done a market working in the day in Gurgaon & had driven up down from Greater Noida chalking up 130 Kms and 4 hours of drive in the chaotic Delhi NCR traffic. Just as I was cooling down myself after a cold shower & ice laden khus sherbet, I got a sms from Vishesh. "Sir Beer today". Vishesh was one of the two Area Managers I had in NCR. "Talk to Sid if he is on". I messaged back. "We are together" texted Vishesh. Both of them had delivered fantastic sales in April & therefore wanted to celebrate. "Ok come over to Greater Noida". I did not want to kill their enthusiasm.

Thirty-five minutes later, both of them were at the gate of my condominium. I lumbered down the steps in my flip flops, T shirt & Shorts. I shared a very friendly rapport with both of them off work while maintaining a Manager Reportee relationship while on work. It helped all of us as the atmosphere was always light & both stood up whenever business required them to do so. Sid's Hyundai Santro was chilling & it provided a perfect environment to enjoy some Chilled Beer Cans in typical Dilli ishtyle called "Car–O- Baar". Sid was driving around the wide empty landscaped roads of Greater Noida which was made doubly enjoyable with the music & Kingfisher. As I was dipping into my 2nd Can of Kingfisher, my Nokia E71 buzzed.

"Nuts Calling", the screen showed. Nuts as he was fondly called for his eccentricity was our Business Head & General Manager of India operations of Chocolates vertical. Mars in India that time had three businesses of Pet Food called Pedigree, Gums by the name Wrigley & the Chocolate business. Mars Inc had finally decided to focus on India Market with all their might & resources with all of their brands & businesses. Growth of India Business had garnered World-wide attention. No week passed by where we did not have a High Profile Visitor from Europe, America or Middle East in one of the three verticals. Preparing for these Visitors had become a part of the routine as wanted to showcase the work which we were doing in India.

"Hello, Sir," I said gathering my senses. Within a split second the iconic scene of the blockbuster movie "Dil Chahta Hai" starring Aamir, Saif & Akshaye was playing in my head. I instantaneously became Saif Ali Khan as I could barely mumble & there was a Forehand, Backhand, Volley, Smash from the other side. The intensity of the strokes was making me numb accentuated by one half cans of Kingfisher. I was able to make little sense of what Nuts was shouting at the top of his voice. I was able to gather that some major screw up happened somewhere. Sales Director of UK, David for Wrigley was visiting Gurgaon. I was not aware about his visit plan & his route with zero inkling of the stores that he would be visiting. He wanted to see the Wrigley placement at impulse shelves at the Cash Counter in Modern Trade stores & he went over to one of Reliance Smart Store in Sector 29 Gurgaon. Murphy's law "anything that can go wrong will go wrong" struck.

Ten years back India used to have a serious power cut problem. It got accentuated in summers & Gurgaon power distribution lines were notorious for failing for many hours. Due to the searing heat & the voltage fluctuations, the dairy chiller at the Reliance store had conked off. We did not have a permanent promoter at the store but was frequented by a merchandiser. Murphy was smiling as the merchandiser had visited a day prior to the power issue & the visit of David happened on the same day after the merchandiser. In order to save whatever could be saved, the staff at the store had shifted all the products in the dairy chiller to the normal bay shelves but this they had done after few hours by which the chocolates, Mars, Galaxy & Snickers had melted completely.

The next morning, dairy chiller was repaired & the all stock was shifted back again from the shelves. Since the chocolates were in a liquid form, they started freezing in the same shape of ginger displayed on a vegetable cart. All possible combinations of geometric shapes chocolates were present in the contraption unit on the wall of the dairy chiller. David was an avid photographer, so he used his skills in capturing all the nooks & corners of the chocolates & sent all the pictures to Nuts. Mars Inc had made a conscious decision not to enter India for decades because India had a reputation for poor infrastructure quality at retail stores. They valued Quality over any amount profit. David's photographic skills could change the narrative at the global headquarters because this happened in a high disposable income cluster of Gurgaon next to the capital of India in a fancy modern trade outlet. They would shudder to think of the product quality in the bylanes of India in the thousands of Mom & Pop stores.

While I was getting a pasting from Nuts, I could hear continuous ticks on my phone. I shifted to hands free & saw missed Calls from the Business Development Head & recently joined National Sales Manager. They had probably got the taste of the medicine which was getting administered to me like a soft drink. "Give me some time I will handle this & I'm sorry for what happened", I answered Nuts. Nuts somehow trusted me explicitly. We shared a very strong bond because he had tremendous faith in me. I had to do something because there was no way I was going to lose this trust.

Instinctively I told Sid, "Let's go to the store". "Sir, it's 7.30 pm, we are 65 Kms away. Driving at this rush hour in Delhi traffic will take us minimum two hours & the store closes at 9.30 pm", Sid answered doubtfully. "Does not matter, we will try". I ordered. So here were three of us with half beer cans in our hands which now was tasting extremely bitter & all the high that Kingfisher had given came crashing down like Kingfisher Airlines. Sid converted his Santro into a Ferrari driving at breakneck speed, cruising like a bee in the maze-like evening rush hour traffic. Meanwhile I was working on my phone assuaging both the Business Development Manager & the National Sales Manager that I would salvage the situation in the next two hours. I called up the Sales Officer of Gurgaon, Pankaj. I told him "Just go right now to the store & hold the shutter from closing till we enter & collect all the melted chocolates in a box to be stashed away in defective product category."

"Sir, they are closing, lights are getting put out", Neeraj called frantically.

"Stand below the shutter & don't move till I come", pat came my reply.

We reached just at the nick of the time. All the chocolates had been collected by Neeraj in a box. I asked the Store Manager to remove all our Chocolates from the Shelf & we could replace it next Morning from the Distributor. He was on a trip of his own & did not agree. He said all chocolates are in the same condition. "What is your problem, it sells in this form only in summers. Customers will buy it & put in their refrigerator", he taunted. I said, "We are Mars. There is zero compromise on quality". Since I was not carrying my wallet, I asked Sid for his credit card. "Bill everything, we will pay". Everyone was zapped. I got 543 units of chocolates billed in all form, size, shapes. "What will you do with these?", store manager asked. "I will throw them". I responded.

The Company has 5 Principles & every Associate lives by those. Quality, Responsibility, Mutuality, Efficiency & Freedom. I had heard stories how the Pet Food business in India has picked up thousands of suspected Salmonella infected bags at MRP from the market & burned them.

I called up the National Sales Manager on my drive back from Gurgaon to Greater Noida. "Manit, it's sorted". He was shocked to know that I was in Gurgaon. He offered me to come over to his place for dinner which I politely refused. I reached home at 1.30 AM & sent a Mail to Nuts with images of empty shelves with a SOP of how to deal with such a situation in the Future. Next morning, I reached the Head Office in Gurgaon to be welcomed by the Management Team for the Quick & Decisive Action. I was later awarded as the "Most Engaged Associate" with a trip to Beijing & Shanghai to visit Chocolate Manufacturing sites in China.

Moral of the Story: Engagement is an emotional connect, it can never be bought with a perk or salary. When you are truly engaged, you don't look at your watch.

Passion!

Greater Noida. June 2021

"Death toll goes below 1000" read the headline of Times of India. Entire country irrespective of socio-economic class had gone through hell of the second wave of Covid-19. There was hardly anyone who did not know of someone passing away due to unavailability of beds, oxygen or remdesivir injections. I was among the lucky ones who did not get the infection home which was a blessing as the family was healthy. However, the underlying stress due to the uncertainty of future of Retail sector was causing some sleepless nights. I was working as the Chief Operating Officer with Iconic Fashion Retail but I knew that it be nearly impossible for the company to pay salaries because of the closure of the stores & even if they could muster some amount of cash, it had to rightfully go to the front-end staff who were facing a dire survival situation.

One Saturday morning, my phone buzzed. Truecaller showed "Ninay Calling". My mind was racing & it took me fraction of a second to recognize the person as the Leadership Hiring Manager at Clickdeal. "Is Clickdeal alive", I questioned to myself. "Hello

Priyaranjan", how are you. Said Ninay. I responded with pleasantries & the normal phone conversation covid-19 protocol asking about health of family etc. This was not the first time that someone from Clickdeal had approached me, but nothing had materialised in the previous conversations. Therefore, I was taking this conversation quite casually because I knew at the back of mind that this would probably lead to nowhere. "We want to open offline stores," remarked Ninay. This got me really interested as I heard every single work post this comment with rapt attention. "I would be keen, let me send across the resume," I answered.

Ninay called up couple of days later fixing up a video chat with the CEO of Clickdeal. He was the doyen of the start-up eco system & proverbial OG of all new age founders. I had rehearsed my introduction & how I would lead the interview by finishing my statement at the tip of an intriguing topic thus leading him into asking a question for which I was prepared. The discussion went off really well & I surprised him by sending him a deck of what I thought should be the contours of the offline format of stores. I spent the next couple of weeks in visiting Sarojini Nagar market, often referred as the Mecca of Street Fashion in India, taking copious notes on how tiny stores cramped in spaces of 10 ft x 15 ft traded merchandise worth Lacs every day. I took mental note of how idiot proof displays were done by the retailers to increase the display space & simultaneously cut down the transaction time. It is a case study in itself how real business operates in India.

The second round of discussion with the CEO was more detailed running into late hours of a Sunday evening. He seemed convinced by my pitch that I was the right guy to lead this business but was guarded enough not to give out what was running through his mind. In the next couple of days, I was asked to give references which I readily provided. "What you sow, so shall you reap", the adage was true for me as I sent a Whatsapp text to couple of my ex-managers & supervisors & they wholeheartedly agreed to put in a good word for me. I was asked for my salary slips which made me convinced that I was going in to start a business venture from scratch like an intrapreneur. However, it was short lived because I was informed by Ninay that there would another round of discussion.

The final discussion was a short one but I felt it was more a reaffirmation from the other side to be triply sure about the hiring decision. I felt good because if they were giving so much time in hiring, it could only imply the high importance attached with the position. Finally, the job offer was rolled out to me & it was gleefully accepted by me. As soon as I signed on the dotted line, I was sent a meeting request for the next steps.

I thought that the first call will be an ice breaker, which was immediately proved wrong as the demand from the CEO was to open the first store in Ninety days before Diwali of 2021. I was shaken up by this aggressive time line but decided to take this as a challenge. The stage was set up for failure. I did not have a single member in the team nor there was any time to hire. I did not know where the store would open, what will it look like, what will I stock up to sell, where will I recruit the team. While I was processing the enormity of the challenge, I was also supposed to navigate the complex standard operating procedures of an E Commerce where nobody understood physical retail but thought themselves to be the masters of the trade. I knew I was up against an improbable task but decided not to fret about the timeline instead focus on the building blocks & the steps.

The basic necessity for any retail store is the physical space or the location. Since I was in my notice period, I could not actively solicit agents & brokers for properties. I needed to find someone who would do it immediately. A guy called Sahyadri had worked with me when I was with Pantaloons in Kolkata. He had lost his job in the pandemic & was sitting idle at his home. I called him up & offered him a three-month contract to work with me. He readily agreed & we started scouting locations. While the location hunting was on, I desperately needed someone who could help me with sourcing the merchandise or the stock for the store. I called up my friends to seek help. They laughed at me saying how could you do sourcing for one store at this time of the year when all the factories & vendors have finished sending the season stock. Undeterred, I marched on thinking, there had to be some solution.

Dharmender. Not the movie star but one of my old acquaintances from Pantaloons was cooling his heels in Ludhiana after being laid off during the pandemic. I called him, explained him that I could offer a three-month contract, to which he readily agreed & got down to making the plan for merchandising the store. The next task was what shape, identity & form would the store would take. I was very clear from the start that there had to be serious differentiation from the existing players in the market to get the customers step in to the store. I had no clue about how store design was done. I banked on my good karma again seeking help from a direct report in Pantaloons. He patiently explained to me the process of store design & after hearing me out about the super audacious plan of opening a new store without location, merchandise, identity in ninety days advised me to give this project on turnkey basis to 4D consultants in Bangalore. He agreed to set up an introduction call with the team of 4D.

Nagaraj & Surender from 4D team told me that it takes 8 months for them to make a mock store or a prototype of a new concept when the retailer had all the resources & here I was asking them to open a store in 8 weeks from absolute scratch. They asked me to send them a design brief. I had a blueprint of the store already in my head through my multiple visits to Sarojini Nagar market. I reverted to the brief in 15 minutes which shocked them as the normal TAT in Organizations for this will be 3 weeks. The three building blocks of who will find the store, what will be put in store & how will the store look was WIP fifteen days ahead of my official joining date. Sahyadri was coordinating with brokers & agents for locations in Gurgaon, Faridabad, Ghaziabad, Sonipat, Palwal, all withing 50 km radius of Delhi. He sent me a picture with coordinates of a prospective site in Gandhi Nagar market of Ghaziabad. It looked interesting from the google location & the available pictures. I was on the way in next fifteen minutes & reached the location in 45 minutes. The market looked half closed as if it was suffering from a disease, which in fact it was due to Covid induced multiple lockdowns. This market was one of the oldest street fashion markets of Ghaziabad. The site was originally a sweet shop but it closed down due to a dispute between the partners operating the place.

I walked up & down the street, spent close to an hour, feeling the vibe of the place, doing basic enquiries about the footfalls in the area. The road was teeming with at least twenty-five shops selling street fashion & first copy footwear. I liked the place & asked Sahyadri to go ahead. Simultaneously, I worked with Dharmendar on the assortment & made the buy plan of stocks. I was also chasing 4D furiously much to their irritation. 1st September 2021 was the day when I was supposed to join Clickdeal. The morning saw torrential rains soon converting roads into small lakes. I started driving on the Noida Greater Noida Expressway but soon realized that reaching Gurgaon Sector 67 where Clickdeal's office was located was a near impossible task. I hopped onto Delhi Metro from Okhla Bird Sanctuary Station. The metro was deserted as India was still recuperating from the delta wave devastation forcing all offices to shift to work from home.

Meanwhile, I got a text from the CEO that he was making a U-turn at Vasant Vihar after getting stuck on the road for an hour. I walked into an empty Clickdeal office. Sahyadri had flown in from Kolkata & Dharmendar had travelled from Ludhiana. The three musketeers had joined together. I had scheduled a call with 4D & the CEO of Clickdeal on the first look of the format. The call finished & I asked the CEO if he would like to visit the site selected by me. Meanwhile I helped in getting both my colleagues place to stay in Gurgaon. The next day the CEO came down to Ghaziabad &

approved the location. I could understand from his tentative steps inside the site that he was seeing something like this for the first time. While the audacious goal was taking some shape, one afternoon I got a frantic call from Sahyadri. "Sir, the landlord of the site has given the property to some other party." This was a bombshell I was not prepared for.

"What do we do now?" I asked him. "There is a ready to move property in Aligarh," he replied. I thought for a second & decided to go to Aligarh same evening. I sat in my Jeep Compass at 4.30 pm & started from Greater Noida taking the Agra Expressway. The drive was not smooth as it crossed the small hamlet of Khair which had a 1 km long traffic jam. I reached Aligarh at 7.30 pm & started visiting the shortlisted sites. I did not like any of them. I was extremely tired & dejected after I finished looking up the last site in Aligarh. The drive through the dark & pot holed state highway was scary. But all that what running through my mind was what would happen next. I was one more day short with no location in place.

Moral of the Story: Passion is an inexplicable emotion which does not require external stakeholders to fuel

Fortitude!

Greater Noida. June 2021

Continued from Tales of Sales (TOS10)

Time was running out. I was already in the first week of September with no location in hand to open the first Clickdeal store. This was a moment of abject disappointment and despair. I felt powerless and helpless. I have always looked to a few movies as sources of inspiration in my daily life. Suddenly I remembered the scene in the movie "Uri" when Major Vihaan played by Vicky Kaushal is ordered not to cross the border in the chopper & after few seconds of blanking, he thinks of a Plan B. While I was finalizing the property in Ghaziabad, I had noticed a next door property with huge shutters but it was closed. I immediately instructed Sahyadri to get me the property.

While this was my wish & it was an arrow shot in dark, it just hit the bulls eye. The Landlord agreed. I was there at the site in the next 60 minutes. Since I could not wait for the CEO to visit this place, I made videos of the location & sent it to him for approval. This was a god given location which was an apparel store in the past & thus was constructed in a manner & form which we liked. This would reduce the civil work to minimum positively impacting lead times. The Letter of Intent was signed in a week's time. This was one major hurdle out of the way but I was getting this strong vibe that I would be able to pull off the impossible task. Simultaneously I suggested something to 4D Consultants, something which they had never heard. Their way of working with all International & Domestic Clients meant developing prototypes for everything, working on identity, colour, theme, developing a model of fixtures & then going for making the layouts & civil, electrical plans & final mock ups.

I told Nagaraj & Surender that there was no time to do mock ups. Clickdeal had filed a Draft Red Herring Prospectus for IPO where they had spelled out their Omni Channel fashion retail plans which meant building a physical store network. Since the IPO was expected in next 120 days in the good days of the start-up funding cycle, the store had to open within that time frame. While they understood but said it was an impossible task which they had never done in their collective 50 years of experience. But I was adamant, since we were not making a headway in discussion, I persuaded them to take step by step & cut down process time at every step. Couple of days later they sent me a draft layout. Layout is a basic plan of the store which is the building block for the entire structure. Therefore, it requires a lot of discussion & deliberation resulting in at least three weeks of turnaround time for decision. I reverted to them in flat three minutes because I just knew what I wanted. I had the mental map of the store engrained in my head which meant easier explanations & rapid decision making. They were shocked & pleasantly surprised at my audacity.

After putting the building blocks of actual store in place, my focus shifted to procuring the merchandise which was the actual make or break. Customers do not pay for the ambience, experience or service, they only pay for the product. Therefore, all the effort of putting up the store would go down the drain if we failed to get in the right merchandise at right price. Everybody knows about the diversity of India but it is also exemplified in the way some of the cities are known for a specific type of apparel. Like Lucknow is known for chikan work, Varanasi is famous for silk, Jaipur manufactures eighty percent of the readymade ethnic wear for women. My first stop was Jaipur. We had a list of the best vendors of Clickdeal who sold online on Clickdeal's website. Dharmender was the product expert but had never worked in ethic wear for women. So here were two men, one of them had no clue about sourcing for women fashion & the other one had very little idea about specific trends in the market for women.

But it did not deter us. We badgered on driven by our maniacal desire to get the best garments at the most affordable price for Clickdeal customers. We visited ten vendors in Jaipur, finalized the styles, took pictures & came back dog tired to Delhi after spending two days in the heat & dust of Jaipur city. We made similar trips to Agra, famous for its footwear. We travelled to Ahmedabad & Vadodara because there are quality manufacturers of denim in these towns. Every second day we were roaming the streets of Gandhi Nagar Market in East Delhi, considered to be the biggest

Readymade garment wholesale market in India. I was surprising myself with the zeal, passion & craziness each day as to how I woke up motivated each morning after a tiring & demoralizing previous day. I discovered many brands of Bharat which were more popular than Levis. One may not have heard the names of Sparky or Flu but listening to their stories of evolution & growth taught me importance of real consumer feedback, understanding & action.

Our make or break point for the Clickdeal Store was the winter wear (Jackets, Sweaters, Sweatshirts) because we were planning the store opening in the month of November & December. The only city in India where winter wear is manufactured in abundance is Ludhiana. We camped in Ludhiana for 5 days, visiting ten manufacturers & selected the merchandise. This was a herculean effort & the effects of non-stop physical travel & mental stress was finally beginning to show upon me.

Lots of processes of actually building a concept from scratch was absolutely new to me. I was learning & performing on the fly. Things that one takes for granted in life in established organizations becomes excruciatingly hard when you have to do it with your own hands in a start-up. Setting up an IT system to making product & vendor codes, generating bar codes, releasing Purchase Orders & finally inwarding the stock was more difficult than all what I had accomplished by now. This required alignment & cooperation of larger pool of stakeholders from the normal business of Clickdeal. They operated at their decided TAT levels which meant delay of Purchase Orders resulting in vendors selling off the selected stock which we had picked painstakingly over the last thirty days. Undeterred with maniacal zeal I repeated the entire process of travel, selection, ordering ensuring availability of right stock for the consumer. One afternoon while I was inspecting the civil works at the site, a consignment of Shirts from a vendor called Robin Rider arrived at the store. The driver of the tempo unloaded it on the doorstep, took the receiving and sped away. There were two hundred & fifty boxes of shirts tied together in fives.

The warehouse was on the second floor leading from a narrow staircase. We had only one housekeeping help, manager & one staff & myself. We could not leave the boxes on the floor so all three of them started to take box sets one by one but it would have meant seventeen trips for each one of them to climb two floors with weight. Spur of the moment, I decided to form a chain to throw up box sets one level at a time. So here I was the Business Head of Clickdeal ensuring the inventory was safely stored. This remains my favourite sub story in the entire Clickdeal tenure. Slowly but surely inventory started to arrive from all vendors. We picked up stock from nearly seventy-five vendors across the length & breadth of the country in sixty days. Endless Days & sleepless nights were spent in following up with vendors, directing the truck drivers & recruiting the warehouse team. While all this was on, I needed a reliable Store Manager. I posted a job on LinkedIn & got hundreds of responses. Anurag was based in Bangalore & wanted to relocate to North. He was recommended highly by one of my acquaintances in Pantaloons. I had a quick chat with him & decided to get him onboarded.

He turned out to be the greatest help in ensuring timely opening of the store.

The civil work was completed & furniture work with site carpentry was going on in full swing. There was some shape & form emerging of the first Clickdeal store. But something was bothering me big time. I was not able to put my finger on the big reason, "Why will the customer visit us? How do I differentiate & give them a reason to come shopping to our store?"

I have always been an ardent admirer of Indian Mom & Pop store owners. They are real entrepreneurs who operate businesses with tight margins & working capital & still earn profits. They are a real-life lesson to all new age startups. My hypothesis for their success was based on three principles. They knew their customer inside out with their names & needs, often garnishing the shopping experience with special discounts. I had to do something special & exciting for the customers to shop at Clickdeal store repeatedly considering that Clickdeal was not naturally inviting considering its chequered past. One day I had to go a railway station to drop off my relative. I saw a dilapidated weighing machine in one corner which used to be an attraction for kids to hop on to its platform, insert one rupee coin, wait for the wheel to spin & stop, hear the typical dispensing sound & take away the small ticket bearing the weight & the daily horoscope.

I had got my cue. My first differentiator was ready in my mind. I would install this machine at the entrance to the store and we would request the customer to hop on the machine, insert a coin & they would get a ticket with a customized promotion. The tall red colour machine was bound to recreate childhood memories in everyone's head. The difficulty was the procurement of this machine as Indian Railways had removed it from its platforms. I placed a request through IndiaMart & got the contact of the manufacturer located in Delhi. I paid a visit to his place immediately and he was surprised hearing out my concept but promised to help me get one machine as there was only three available with one of them going to Mr Ambani's house & other one was blocked by Mr. Bill Gates office as per the manufacturer.

Still, this wasn't sufficient, as I wanted to replicate the discount given by the local retailer at the point of billing but it was impossible to execute from a controls point of view in an organized retail store. I was travelling to Ahmedabad one day & saw a brand-new Coca Cola vending machine at the airport. Vending Machines in India is still an enigma. Everyone wants to use it but does not know how to or does not find one easily. I connected with a smart vending machine vendor called Daalchini & created a proposition for the customer who shopped with us to pick any product of their choice free from the vending machine through a coupon code given at the time of billing. I was relatively sure that consumers would love this experience as no retailer was giving this kind of service & recreating the warmth & comfort of street shopping in organized trade format.

While the service differentiators were settled, I was still grappling with the reason for customers to visit as us as sustenance of the format depended on word of mouth. One day while roaming in Mall of India, I stumbled upon an idea of creating a big shoe section, denim section & jacket section. If we could crack couple of propositions to stand out, it would be a big driver in ensuring repeat customer visits to the store. I got after the design agency's life to give me a concept to display larger than life sections of the above categories. They came up with beautiful three-dimensional sectional images which enhanced the look and feel of the store. I came up with one more innovations of creating customized denim by steam pressing stickers which I sourced from the bylanes of Gandhi Nagar after searching for the same for two days. It was a simple but an effective memory tool which I picked up from the Levis tailoring shop concept in their exclusive brand outlets.

I tried my level best but in spite of my efforts we stepped into December month for opening of the store. Now came the most difficult part of ensuring eye catching displays through visual merchandising & price navigation. Since we had sourced merchandise from seventy vendors, it was impossible to establish correct price laddering so I decided to make pricing cuts of 199,399,599,799,999 & put a red colour sticker on all 5000 pieces so that it became easy for the consumer to shop. We slept three nights in ensuring the stickers were put & the stock was merchandised to present a great looking store to the consumers. My phone kept buzzing all the time as we were simultaneously looking for a franchisee to operate the store as the FDI rules in retail prevent a foreign funded Multi branded retail from operating a store directly. Unfortunately, Clickdeal fell into this category. Finally, we got hold of a guy to give us a name & GST number in return for a handsome amount paid every month.

The D-Day was fast approaching & I was getting restless as we had not started any marketing activation to popularise the store in the catchment. I did not want any run of the mill boring activation. It had to be something which customers would stop & take a selfie with. Out of many whacky and crazy things done in this store, I got an 8 Feet real life 10 Oz denim tailored and installed. It looked magnificent. Soon there was a traffic jam on the road outside the store as passer byes stopped to click pictures. The objective that I had set out to achieve of catching everyone's attention was accomplished. The store opened on 1st Jan exactly one hundred twenty days after I joined Clickdeal. I surmounted unimaginable hurdles & battled unbelievable odds to see that day. My biggest rewards was losing seven kilograms in the process & gaining a perpetual salt pepper frizzy hair look. My phone beeped, there was a Whatsapp forward from the CEO on his conversation with his mother, who had texted him "Mazaa aa gaya dekh kar".

Moral of the Story: When you really want something very badly, the elements of the nature support you in achieving the objective (*Shah Rukh Khan in Om Shanti Om*)

Audacity!

Gurgaon. Aug 2019

It was late evening on the eve of Independence Day. I was sitting in my corner office in Sector 14 Gurgaon trying to listen to Sriram who was patiently trying to explain the loyalty program running at Iconic stores. I had recently joined the company as the Chief Operating Officer of Iconic Fashion Retailing Pvt Ltd. Iconic had 22 stores across India through which it retailed premium International Fashion brands like Tommy Hilfiger, Calvin Klein, GANT, Jack & Jones, Antony Morato etc. I had left my previous job at Pantaloons as the Vice President Sales & Operations where I was responsible for managing over 150 Stores generating a revenue of 1400 Crore Plus. Lot of people told me it was a suicidal move but then I have always believed that in order to understand how deep the water is, you need to jump. One can never become a great swimmer unless you navigate unfamiliar waters.

Coming back to the story, I was yawning by the time Sriram finished his laboriously made powerpoint slides. I was apologetic for my disinterested body language but I could not help it as I knew the loyalty program which was running was nothing but a sham. They were paying 40 Lacs per year to an agency to run a program where the Customers were redeeming point value worth 2 Crore annually with no proof of driving repeat purchases. In fact, they had doled out points worth 4 Crore the previous year with abysmal rate of returning customers. In my head the current loyalty program was a dead horse which the consumers had rejected because everyone is bored with the concept of point system with zero transparency as the value of the points could vary from 25 Paisa to One Rupee for a point. But this conversation took me back two years to a stormy Kolkata evening.

Dark clouds with lightening were gathering over the sky as I preened through the window of the conference room of East Zone Office located in the business district of Salt Lake. Those dark clouds were not only circling the Kolkata sky but also the Pantaloons business. They were in the shape of extreme competition from formats called Central & Shoppers Stop. Pantaloons had an iconic store in the temple city of Bhubaneswar on the main Janpath road called the shopping paradise of Bhubaneswar. The Pantaloons store was so unique in nature that the folklore said that when it opened way back in 2008, people would just walk in to the store to go up & down on the escalator because it was the only escalator that time in the city and watching a staircase moving was a big attraction. The brand had a golden run for nearly nine years with no competition. However, three months back, Future Group had entered Bhubaneswar through a format called Central which boasted of four floors of endless assortment with more than five hundred brands in Men, Women, Kids fashion & lifestyle. We were no match for

Central. Resultant we lost our staff, our customers & our business big time. In short, we were rogered with no place to hide.

Buoyed by it's success in Bhubaneswar, Central was eyeing Kolkata city which was jewel in Pantaloons crown. They were getting a seventy thousand square feet store ready on the outskirts of Kolkata in Rajarhat. This was bothering me as I knew Bhubaneswar 2.0 was in the offering. But I did not know the way to give a meaningful & befitting response to competition. All of us were doing something or the other but deep down in my heart I knew it was more a tick box exercise. While I was absorbed in deep thought, I was taking a post dinner walk in the apartment complex Rosedale Garden in New Town with my son & narrating him a story. He was in his own playful mood while I was very sombre. Suddenly he asked, "Dad, why are the compound walls so high?". I explained him that it was done so that it would be difficult for people to jump in & and out of the complex from the wall. Something struck me as I was speaking the sentence. "We should make it difficult for customers to jump out of Pantaloons compound into Central compound". I had my cue.

Without wasting any time, I started designing the contours of the program. It meant designing a new loyalty program where the customer would be locked in with us. I was thinking about an audacious plan of charging a subscription amount from the customer. Back in 2017, subscription especially in brick & mortar retail was a novel concept. Few had tried, failed & stopped the experiment. But I was adamant of seeing this one through. My biggest concern was the flight of the top spenders at Pantaloons. I had to somehow create an obstruction in this flight. Additional discount was an easy way out but I wanted to ask them upfront subscription amount to enrol into the program, commit & then get a discount. I coined the program as Insignia. The concept of Insignia was simple but its execution was difficult. We would offer a customer ten percent additional discount for three sixty-five days from the day of enrolment over & above any promotion running in the store. In return they had to take Insignia membership by paying nine hundred & ninety nine upfront.

I did all permutation & combinations and arrived at all possible scenarios. A few days later the CEO visited Kolkata & I explained this program to him. He rubbished it saying we would leak margin badly & our profitability would suffer. I had anticipated this reaction, therefore I switched to plan B creating all possible scenarios starting from not worst case but pathetic case. I had thought of improbable situations which in this model was not making a loss. The CEO was flummoxed though generally he was extremely sharp with numbers, this one had stumped him. He tossed & turned all permutations & combinations and very reluctantly admitted that it seemed a fool proof plan which had the potential of turning around Pantaloons fortunes. He sent an email to entire leadership team stating how this initiative of Insignia launch could be the most significant event in the history of Pantaloons. I was overjoyed with the confidence reposed in my plan & I got down to fine tuning it. The day we launched it in five stores, we did not see any enrolment.

While it was deflating but I knew we had to keep at it. The only metric I tracked for the next 90 days was Insignia enrolment. Slowly the tide started to turn & conversations about the program benefits started with the customers. The success of the program depended on the manner in which it would be explained to the customer. Thankfully the team started to run with the Insignia baton after a very slow start but slowly & surely, Insignia had started to make a difference. We had made a small hedge around our stores which disabled the customers to walk out freely to Central. One always remembers what one spends & not what one earns. Therefore, the program subscribers would always visit Pantaloons as the first choice because they knew that had invested in Insignia & wanted their ROI. What started as an experiment for few stores in Kolkata, expanded to the entire country with each store entrance and the cash bay of each and every of 350+ Pantaloons stores proudly displays the Insignia loyalty program.

Coming back to the story in Gurgaon at Iconic, I knew very clearly that we needed a hook for the customers to come back to our stores to visit as we were selling brands which were available in the brand exclusive brand outlets (EBOs) in the same shopping mall or the city. While I had the knowledge and the success experience of Insignia in Pantaloons, this one required a completely different thought. I thought long and hard for many days before coming up with a plan. This one was 10x more audacious than Insignia. I wanted to a charge nine thousand nine hundred and ninety-nine as upfront subscription amount. This was some investment that we were seeking from the customer. But in return I wanted to make an offer which no shopper could refuse. I realised that shopping in Iconic stores was more snob value for the international brand that one was wearing which not just remained with what the customers were wearing but with the what accessories they were carrying. One such nondescript accessory is luggage. We offered ten percent additional discount over and above anything running as a promotion in store with a Tommy Hilfiger Mid-Size hard top luggage with retail price of fourteen thousand five hundred as immediate return gift and a five thousand rupee birthday voucher on select brands in the store.

The next task was to find an appropriate and reliable vendor who could supply this. I got in touch with a vendor who sold Tommy Hilfiger bags in India. They were based in Indore and readily agreed with our proposal. While this was all taped up, I coined the program as "Iconic by Choice" and went up to the CEO who was the founder promoter of Iconic with the proposal. He was shocked and surprised with the plan and immediately started playing the devil's advocate stating that it would be impossible to extract such a high value as commitment from the customer. I reinitiated my plan of Pantaloons of creating improbable scenarios and the proposal started moving back and forth from the tables of CEO and CFO. Hectic consultations followed and nothing moved.

After two months, I made the CEO agree to try it as a pilot in two worst performing stores. The deal was, if it did not work, I would shut my trap and if it did, we would launch it everywhere. Rigorous follow ups ensued and the D-Day arrived in Bhopal and Pune stores. It made me immensely happy to get the first sign up done after a lot of efforts but I noticed that the way of pitching the program was incorrect. It was getting presented as a promotion offer which would defeat the purpose of the program. I came back to the drawing board and prepared an extensive script focusing "Iconic by choice" tag line. It was supposed to be presented as the famed Jet Privilege platinum card or the American Express platinum card which talks about elevating the experience of the customers without explicitly mentioning the discounts. I followed the same strategy and it worked in both Pune and Bhopal. Just when we were getting ready to launch it pan India, Covid struck smashing all my plans.

As retail sector started to open up post the first wave, the footfalls to the stores were abysmal. It made great sense to launch the program as the walkins were limited so the only way to survive was to upgrade the customer's ticket size of their shopping cart. We launched the program full scale during Covid and the results were on expected lines. We ran out of luggage bags in the third week of launch of the program. The staff realised it was a sure shot ticket to repeat customer visits. The program got in additional revenue during Covid which proved to be a lifeline. "Iconic by Choice" stands at the gate of every Iconic store today and is continuously driving increased visits of customers to the stores which is the main objective of any loyalty program.

Moral of the Story: Unless the status quo is challenged with audacity, same inputs will deliver marginally lesser output with time.

Rationality!

Greater Noida. Sep 2023

"Common sense is like deodorant, people who it need most never use it" and it is very common to lose sense and rationality in sales. Thankfully I learnt this lesson very early in my career. The back story dates to the hot summer month of April 2009. It had been just over a month since I had joined United Breweries (maker of iconic Kingfisher beer) as the Branch Sales Manager, Haryana. For the uninitiated, beer is manufactured in brewery and spirits (hard liquor) in distillery.

While the brand and the job looked supremely attractive from the outside considering the IPL connection, Kingfisher Calendar, Kingfisher Airlines, Formula 1 and the yacht parties in Goa, it was an anti-thesis from the inside. I was supposed to be managing the business in Haryana which had an archaic license, auction and contractor system. Alcoholic beverages is a regulated sector which comes under the state excise laws, and therefore, the process and manner to execute sales and distribution varies from state to state. Old timer traders in this business rule the roost as it requires muscle power, political patronage and loads of money.

Beer and Spirits cannot be sold from anywhere and everywhere in Haryana. There are earmarked spots where liquor vends (L2's) are allowed. The number of spots remain more or less the same every year while the operator may change basis the price they bid in the auction. Thus 1st of April may see a new operator in all the shops or some of the shops. The bid price is quoted by entities who may be old in the trade or someone who may have formed partnerships. The bids are then opened and licenses to operate vends is granted for a year by the excise department of the state. Sensible traders put in a price which is reasonable which could fructify into profits after paying the license fee as rent to the excise department and factoring in operating costs along with capex of the vend and paying the companies for their goods.

The companies supply their brands to Wholesalers (L1's) who may or may not own the licenses to operate liquor vends (L2's). It will be incorrect to state that there is no consumer loyalty for the brand in this sector, however brands are highly substitutable as a single reason of Kingfisher not being chilled can change the consumer preference to Haywards. Therefore, the trade enjoys an upper hand in the power equation with the brands. Theoretically if a wholesaler (L1) does not buy a brand X from company Y, there is high probability of brand X not being available in the vend (L2) operated by this particular wholesaler. Therefore, brands in this segment compete with one another to provide stocks to wholesalers. The system is designed in a manner that every wholesaler (L1) needs to take permits for buying from excise department and provide it to the companies for supplying goods. Then there is a fight amongst brands to procure these permits without which no supplies can happen.

And to top it up, every year the labels that are stuck on the bottles are approved by the excise department before which production cannot be completed. The summer of 2009 was different because of a scam getting detected in the excise department, there had been a delay in approvals of labels for brands. Additionally, there was a newbie trader who can be called a start up in today's world had upset the entire apple cart and bid obnoxious prices and procured licenses to operate marquee vends of Gurgaon and Faridabad. He had bid such a high amount that everyone including excise, brands, traders knew that day it would be a losing proposition and since he would necessarily have to pay the license fee for the vend every month, the only place he would default on making the payments would be to the brands. It was known to all that he would go down but he would also take few others with him.

Before we could realize it was already the second week of April with the label approval pending. Beer sales have a direct correlation to temperatures. As the mercury rises, chilled beer bottles start flying off the shelves. The competitors of Kingfisher in Haryana were Haywards and Thunderbolt, both of which had got their labels approved and thus were available in the market. We were not only losing market share badly but also the temper of my Regional Head. Then one fine day the label approval happened and immediately, my manager flew off the handle. There was tremendous pressure to collect permits from wholesalers to supply Kingfisher stocks. I was running from wholesaler to wholesaler to take orders, however desperation in sales means additional discount.

By this time market knew that we were under pressure to collect permits, therefore wholesalers started demanded prices which were 15-20% lower than what we could offer. I informed my Boss about the situation, to which he replied, "We will see later, right now take orders and permits". "But Sir, our payment terms are not clear, order price is not clear, we will be in a soup later", I tried my best to explain to him. There was a volley of abuses from the other side as I was new comer trying to get some sense into a person who had spent twenty years in the liquor trade. As mandated, we got the permits collected and started sending to the brewery. The brewery was under extreme pressure under the sudden surge in demand as it was lying unutilized all this while.

Beer is sold in recycled bottles and there are agents who get the bottles picked from rag pickers, collect it and then send to various brand manufacturing plants. Every brand thus had a different bottle shape and mould to differentiate itself from competition. We had different bottle shapes and colours for our strong, medium and light beer called Kingfisher Strong, Kingfisher Blue and Kingfisher Lager respectively. Kingfisher Strong was 70% of the sales volume which is counter intuitive as globally beer is consumed as a beverage while in India, beer serves the purpose of delivering a high, therefore the preference for Strong beer. The brewery did not have sufficient bottles of Kingfisher Strong as the collection from the agents for empty bottles had been weak. The brewery head called my boss and apprised him of the situation. "Produce Lager and Blue" he responded. The brewery head was surprised but since his KRA was total production, he decided to go as per the instructions.

Soon there was a pile up of Kingfisher Lager and Kingfisher Blue boxes. I was working overtime in the market in collecting the permits. The wholesaler on one hand were putting pressure for discounts but were adamant that only Kingfisher strong be supplied to them. When the pressure to collect permits became unbearable from the top, one of my team mates who was working in the system for ten years, started to pick up permits, telling the wholesalers that we will not despatch the goods and the permits were meant only to appease the management. These permits only specified the quantity of beer to be supplied as the excise department was only concerned with the volume. All the permits were then handed over to the brewery.

We had created a mess for ourselves. We had not confirmed prices from wholesalers, we had given wrong commitment to collect permits, and we had not apprised them that Kingfisher Strong was short in supply. My boss was in regular touch with the brewery head who confirmed receipt of permits and got a go ahead from the Regional Manager to despatch whatever was produced. I again tried to inform my boss about the dangers of the decision but he was in no mood to listen. All of this had taken two weeks to accomplish which meant the month closing had only three days remaining. The flurry of despatches started like a dam was breached. Truck after truck left the brewery with the beer and the permits.

Another complication in this business is the one-way flow of goods. The trucks are despatched with the invoice for the wholesaler and permit from the excise department. It is not possible for the truck to come back to the brewery. It has to be necessarily delivered to the wholesaler who has issued the permit.

As soon as the trucks started arriving at the wholesalers depot, hell broke loose. I was bombarded with angry and abusive calls from wholesalers who were yelling at the top of their voice to take back Kingfisher Lager and Kingfisher Blue as they had categorically informed us that they wanted Kingfisher Strong. Those wholesalers from whom permits were picked with the promise of no despatches were appalled to see trailers carrying 2100 cases reaching their depots. These trucks are not allowed to wait on the main arterial roads so they started parking in front of wholesaler godowns blocking their access. They categorically denied offloading asking us to take back which as per excise rules was not possible. It was stalemate situation leading to casualty of another unrelated party which was the transporters and mainly the drivers and helpers on the trucks and trailers.

They started calling up the Brewery Transport incharge who quickly passed on my number leading to a flood of calls on my mobile incessantly through the night and day. As hours stretched to days and nights, their desperation grew because of the endless wait, no response from us and denial by the wholesalers. They could not move the trucks anywhere on account of the possible penalty by the excise department officials. This was one occasion for the first and last time in my life where I started avoiding and missing calls. In fact, I was under so much pressure from the continuous beeping on m phone that I had to shut it to get some hours of peaceful sleep. The deadlock had to be resolved because it was an untenable situation.

Slowly we requested, begged, cajoled the wholesalers to help us in some manner. We got some success as few trucks got offloaded. The searing heat helped as beer offtake increased in the market leading to huge demand. But all this help from anyone would not come for free. Wholesalers started arm twisting us with their conditions to offload. They wanted a deep discount and delayed payment for the unnecessary and extra stock piled on to them. They were right in their approach and we had no option to give in to their demands to live another day. One day I gathered some courage and told the Regional Manager in front of everyone, "Sir three percentage points of one month market share increases has cost the company ten crores which is equivalent to six months of profit. If only we had done this rationally, we could have still gained one percentage point market share and nor created a insolvable mess". He looked at with flaring nostrils and wide eyes ready to hammer me but it did not perturb me as I was talking logically and sensibly. We had goofed up big time.

Moral of the Story: Irrationality is most times confused for aggression but in reality, it is pure foolishness as any amount of aggression cannot make a bucket hold more water than its capacity.

Improvisation!

Gurgaon. Jan 2008

I parked my black Shahrukh Khan advertised Santro Xing by the roadside in Sector 32 Institutional Area of Gurgaon. As I got down from the car, I saw a magnificent and imposing building with RANBAXY emblazoned on the façade in bold orange colour. I walked in through the main gate after the security checks to see two spanking new silver colour Mercedes parked side by side near the portico. They were the carriers of Malav and Shiv as lovingly called by then Ranbaxy employees. They were the scions of the family with both of them operating as Chief Executives of the company. The receptionist asked my name and asked me to stand in front of the camera and handed over the temporary Identity Card which zipped out from the printer. "Take the elevator, 3rd floor and second left" instructed the receptionist. I was supposed to meet the Sales Head & the Human Resource Manager for an interview.

I had already spent nearly three years in the fuddy duddy system of Hindalco Industries where all my colleagues had the same years of experience as my age.

I was tired of waiting for the next order or lead to fructify from the prospects for Everlast Aluminium roofing sheet. It was an extremely difficult product to sell as it was 6x more expensive than Galvalume which was the preferred material to build industrial sheds. While my sales pitch of Aluminium being a green metal which meant realizing much higher value in the future through recycling was superb but human beings and Organizations think about today's survival compared to fifteen years down the line. Very low order value and sales was the resultant of this price and material disparity which made me quite dejected with the job I was doing. I was looking for an exit when this opportunity with Ranbaxy Global Consumer Healthcare came about as they were looking for an Area Sales Manager based out of Delhi.

I was seated in a big conference room which was intimidating and it got amplified with the entrance of dynamic person who was leading the Sales function for Ranbaxy Consumer. He fired a volley of questions which I though was able to answer satisfactorily as I did get an offer of a job from them. While I was moving out after exchanging pleasantries, the Head of Sales whispered, I'm from the same management institute where you passed out from but much earlier in the 90s. Those words were like a soothing lotion on the skin dryness of a harsh winter as I nearly thought that I had pocketed the offer. I waited for a formal communication from the Human Resource Manager which did not arrive as expected. But she called me after a couple of days to come for joining on the next Monday, however the appointment letter would be given after my meeting with the Business Head. It sounded weird because she was neither denying nor extending the job offer.

However as is often said, beggars can't be choosers which was precisely the state I was in. I reached the same office to be led into the corner cabin of Mr. Kapil who was the Business Head. The magnificence of the Delhi Jaipur highway was clear from the tall window frames as cars zipped on the expressway. While I did not know if they had made up my mind on me, it did seem that this was a final check for the nod from the Head similar to a patriarch approving a would-be groom or bride for marriage. I was asked to wait in one of the cabins while the Human Resource Manager checked with the Business Head on his view. Soon she joined me with a beaming smile congratulating me and handed me the offer letter. "Our North regional office is in Nangli Poona, you are supposed to go there and meet the Regional Sales Manager", she giggled while she said Nangli Poona. It sounded like a place from Chambal ravines and I had no clue of the geography. These were non google map days so I set out from Gurgaon to Nangli Poona which was a village located on the border of Delhi Haryana on the Delhi Chandigarh GT Road. Within a few years a lot of warehouses had sprung up in the vicinity due to its location on the highway.

I had to navigate a lot of u-turns on the busy highway as I kept asking the locals for the location. After a two-hour ordeal I was finally able to locate the regional office of Ranbaxy Consumer Healthcare. It was a very quick briefing from the Regional Manager & I was handed over the Target sheet for Feb & Mar at Product, Distributor & Territory level. The target sheet looked like a trigonometry chapter as it went all above my head. But I had to make a start somewhere, so I enquired about my team.

This was the first Managerial role in my career and my direct reports were 4 Area Sales Executives in (N,E,W,S) Delhi, 1 in Gurgaon who managed Rohtak - Hissar Belt & One 3rd Party Territory Sales Executive based in Ambala managing the GT Belt. The next morning, I took the Delhi Metro and after a couple of interchanges reached Inderlook where a Middle Aged thick moustached man was waiting for me on his Hero Honda Splendour. He was the ASE for North Delhi and was taking me to meet Maharaja Traders, the biggest distributor of Ranbaxy Consumer in Delhi. This was completely new to me from selling Aluminium Roofing Sheets in B2B Industry to an Over the Counter medicine Business. It was a very cold Delhi Morning and the distributors tirade was making it feel colder. One thing which I gathered over the two-hour meeting was that this was a Wholesale driven Business. Hero SKU was a Vitamin Supplement Strip of 10 Capsules of the brand Revital Called a "Patta".

"I can't send my sales representatives to Chemist Stores because their Order Value is small & cost to serve & collect money consumes my margin. Chemist stocks unimaginable width of Product but very less Depth as the nature of Medicine Industry is that Doctors prescribe different Brands for same disease resulting in massive proliferation of Brands. So, a Chemist can never get the complete Assortment from Distributors. They have to rely on Aggregators (Wholesalers) to service them. Any Product which is low on Weight and high on

Value is apt for Wholesaling and that Product gets wings to fly as cost of transportation is low and since I'm the biggest Distributor, I get best schemes which helps to give higher Discounts to Wholesalers who then send the product to Interiors". He meant he was able to do higher Undercutting & there is no Territory Ownership Boundaries. This was my Life Learning which I could juice out from my meeting.

These were non-GST days so differential taxation played a huge role in making products fly from Ludhiana to Delhi to Patna to Lucknow to Kolkata. My next stop in a few days' time was another distributor in Safdarjang Enclave in South Delhi. Guptaji was an affable character who was multitasking with order taking on four mobile phones. He was the distributor for quite a lot of pharmaceutical companies which meant his delivery vehicles traversed Delhi's Ring Road from South to west to North to East. I was amused as he like Maharaja Traders supplying stocks to all possible corners of Delhi while sitting in a corner in South Delhi. The story remained consistent with most of such distributors of Ranbaxy Consumer Healthcare till the time I reached Bhagirath Palace. It is located just about 500 metres from Chandni Chowk Metro Station. This is the mecca for medicine wholesale and a sight to behold looking at the Loaders, Porters, Cart Pullers & the Multi-Millionaire Pharmaceutical Traders of Delhi transacting Millions of Rupees each day from the smallest unimaginable place.

Maiden Pharmaceuticals was our distributor sitting in the hub of Bhagirath Palace. "Sir, my business has collapsed for your company, I was doing nearly 35

Lacs per month which is down to only 15 Lacs as Revital stocks keep flowing into Bhagirath at prices below my cost because of which I'm not able to compete.". "Where are the stocks coming from", I asked a naïve question. "Everywhere from Ludhiana, Patna, Lucknow, Ghaziabad, local Delhi", he answered. "Outside, I understand, but why is it coming from Delhi" my inquisitiveness grew. "Because you have appointed many distributors across Delhi and since they are not able to sell in retail because chemists are getting it cheaper, they are dumping stocks here at nearly their costs to sustain the business. This is killing your retail distribution business as well your whclesale business", he explained. I had just got to understand the genesis of the issue.

Like in most situations of life, problems are never external for organizations. They are created internally because someone's bonus, promotion, target is on the line and they don't think about future repercussions at the present. What the owner of Maiden Pharmaceuticals had elaborated was exactly the reason for stagnancy in Delhi market which the organization was trying to solve by appointing a new Area Manager which was a newly created position.

I had my task cut out as the entire system was positioned in a manner and form to dump stocks and not carry it to the chemist or the retailer. I had to rebuild this machinery but how? I was a newbie in the trade which had big sharks present already. I started to narrow down the issue in the market by visiting retail stores and chemists. Store after store we were rejected with a unanimous view that wholesale price was cheaper than the distributor so they bought from Bhagirath Palace directly. The big issue was the pricing of Revital. It was the pivot for all other brands ordering. I formulated a plan which was outrageous as per market standards which would upset the apple cart completely. I knew I needed a support to start this. One of my direct reports in West Delhi was an enthusiastic young lad which was always willing to go beyond the extra mile for sales.

"I need your help and your distributors help to solve this problem in Delhi once and for all," I asked Kapil. He looked at me through his big spectacles with wide open eyes expecting a bombshell. I wanted the distributor to contribute three percent from his margin of seven percent which I would add to all the existing running schemes and make a proposition for a retailer to buy 10+1 Revital packs at the highest possible discount. The distributor threw a fit when I spoke about this proposal. But mellowed down as I explained that doing higher sales at slightly lower margin was beneficial to him as no one ever takes home the percentages but the absolutes. He agreed after a lot of coaxing. The next day it was pandemonium in the market as I started getting frantic calls from all my direct reports complaining about the scheme launched by Kapil.

I told them to speak to their distributors who should do the same. This worked like a chain reaction within three days, markets in Delhi started to talk only 10+1 Revital. All distributors were forced to change their schemes and had to fork out additional margin from their pocket in order to protect their turf with the danger of another distributor lurking. As this wheel moved faster it completely stopped influx of products from markets outside Delhi resulting in a whopping 20% growth in the market in the year. This 10+1 on Revital continued for a good five years after my tenure reemphasising the importance of that move.

Moral of the story: Treading the downtrodden path will give predictable results, if one has to snatch victort from the jaws of defeat, improvisation is key.

Fearless!

Mumbai. Aug 2018

"Yeh Dil Maange More". This is not just a slogan coined by JWT, an advertising firm for Pepsi in 1998 to target the youth in the mid1990s. This was made hugely popular by Captain Vikram Batra who used this as the battle cry in the Kargil war of 1999. The slogan also has economic principles which says any consumer will desire more good if there are no constraints of budget. The moot point being that unless there is internal motivation, everything else will act at superficial level and the common denominator which provides this motivation is often monetary benefits. I'm being extra careful to point out that some professions and humans are noble not to be touched by this currency.

It was way past midnight in a sweaty August when I noticed that I had been sitting on a recliner sofa thinking about the impending festive season sales for Pantaloons. I had recently moved out of Kolkata to Mumbai after taking the responsibility of Sales & Operations for East & South India. While I was happy to join the leadership team of Pantaloons in the board room, the position I had occupied for three years in

Kolkata was still vacant to be backfilled. Therefore, I was double hatting from Mumbai and spending two to three days a week in Kolkata. The impending Durga Puja period was the make or break event for the year. We had done well in the previous two years on back of an out of box promotion idea but this year seemed an extremely steep climb.

Situation was grim. Last two quarters had seen high Like for Like De-growth. Target achievement was around 75%. Team was demotivated. I was worried and was not able to pin point one big change initiative which would turn around the situation. The festival period is an intense and back breaking period for the front-line staff. When the consumers are shopping to the hearts plenty, there are thousands of sales boys, sales girls who are slogging day and night in order to provide a fantastic experience to the consumer. Often, they become a footnote in the entire story. When they are not able to hit their targets, they have to endure a bad festive period because the incentives they get is the only earning during the year which they spend on themselves. This leads to a negative spiral of demotivation, low energy, and lower sales so on. I had to break this cycle, but how?

Many years back when I was working in Nivea, I heard about the concept of KITA from the Managing Director of Nivea. KITA is an acronym for Kick in the Ass was a part of Herzberg's motivational theory which he published it in 1968. My Managing Director had spun the concept by introducing positive KITA. While the hygiene parameters like salary, working conditions, respect, job role prevented dissatisfaction from the job but they are different from motivators. He made an outrageous plan for a year and announced one month's bonus pay on the condition of achieving the goal. My mind was fixated on that Goa conference and how I could tailor it to my situation. Normal situations call for putting the horse before the cart but I decided to invert it. Going against conventional logic, my plan started germinating in my head which would take out the targets from the equation and thus the pressure.

Targets play havoc in our heads. We all have seen how teams batting first in cricket play with freedom and gay abandon and the same team gets bogged down completely when batting second because there is a target to chase. Yes, there are exceptions to this rule in form of Virat Kohli and Michael Bevan's and Jos Butler's but they are outliers. I wanted to give the feeling of batting first to the team. And my team In East India had over fifteen hundred people who were all looking up to me for some inspiration. I conceived a plan which was never thought or executed in real life. It only existed in imagination where there was a perfect world.

We had to sell close to 35 Lac units of clothes from the Pantaloons stores to meet the target. Task ahead was to deliver Double Digit LFL growth in the Festive Season. It Seemed like Chasing 500 Runs in 50 Overs. But there was unlock possible in chasing 500 runs in 50 overs. What if every batsmen is rewarded for each run irrespective of them scoring one or hundred or more regardless of victory or defeat. This would unshackle them and remove the fear of failure. I copied this concept in my context.

I knew that we would anyways sell 25 Lac units of clothes any which ways, the fight was for the balance 10 Lacs. I made a plan to reward every sales boy or sales girl and managers on the number of garments they sold. The incentive would only be one rupee for a low-price product but it could go upto twenty five rupees for an expensive product. And there would not be any targets. I was banking on the inherent human desire to demand more of good. This was positive KITA. Instead of binding them and putting a leash of a target, I unlocked the chains by letting everyone decide their own target. How much they could earn depended purely on how much they could sell. If one sold only 100 garments during the period, their incentive would be only 200 but if someone would sell 1000 units, they could potentially earn upto seven thousand rupees. This was big money at stake and I was taking a big gamble which could backfire badly in case the overall targets would not happen but incentives would get paid out.

I knew it would require a herculean effort to let this pass through the Finance team and the CEO as Managers are programmed to anticipate the worst possible scenario and paint a pitiable picture. I was walking up and down the aisle of the office in Andheri (East) situated near Saki Naka crossing which was infamous for massive traffic jams every morning and evening. How could I convince them was the question running through my mind. FOMO was my answer. I made an estimated plan basis the current situation and the forecast shook everyone in the management team as this was the only event which could make the company profitable. The trending sales numbers and their trajectory jolted everyone out of slumber and all of them started looking at me for answers. After an hour-long deliberation on possibilities we were reaching nowhere. I was biding my time. I said, "Listen I have a plan but there is a risk of only 50 lacs but if we don't do it we are risking nearly 10 crores of profit".

I could hear a pin drop in the room with deathly silence. "Tell us what is the plan", the CEO asked. I laid the plan open in front of everyone which inculcated the Virat Kohli mindset in all sales boys and girls. Since there was no option left, or I did not leave any option on the table, I got an in principle nod to execute with a soft message about my responsibility for the same. I had never shied away from putting my neck on the block, therefore it did not affect me because I just knew it will work. Motivated and roaring sales boys and girls can sell anything to consumers. Such is the power they hold when they are talking and convincing them. When I discussed it with my team and direct reports, they had their mouth wide open.

No one was able to fathom as to how there could be an incentive without targets. While all seemed hunky dory it was extremely important to roll it out in a proper manner to effectively juice out 100% of the idea. We made an elaborate arrange at newly opened Westin Hotel in Newtown Kolkata where Managers of all Pantaloons stores gathered along with some members of the leadership team with the CEO in attendance. After an hour of boring motivational speeches, it was time for me to take the centre stage. I built the story citing the example of how Pakistan won the 1992 cricket world cup. They were down and out and stayed in the tournament through a freak match there they could score only 74 runs but still drew the match as rain gods intervened. It's history how they bounced back like roaring tigers and played every match without fear of losing resulting in their winning the coveted trophy. "We are down but not out, we are tigers and when tiger takes two steps back, it is not because of fear but for readying to attack", I thundered on stage to a rousing reception. I held on the incentive plan declaration to the last slide on my presentation which made the entire room impatient. I could sense the uneasiness which is exactly I wanted.

"This year during Durga Puja, there will not any targets. Like we are giving consumers choice to choose their own gift basis how much they buy from us, we are leaving the choice to you, how much you want to earn this festive. It is your and your team's hunger which will decide the amount you pocket in the next 45 days. We will launch a per piece incentive without any conditions without any limitation". I announced. It tool precise forty five seconds for everyone to realise the enormity of my declaration. Murmurs started leading to cross talking with expressions of disbelief culminating into a rapturous reception and standing ovation. One hand rose and asked, "Are you saying Sir, there is no target this year for Pujo". I nodded and added "you decide how much you want to earn and that's your target". As I got off the stage to click pictures with all the team members, I felt like a celebrity as many of them asked for selfies.

The CEO was taken aback at this massive reaction and could not believe what she had just witnessed. The next couple of days were spent in taping up all other activities before the D-Day arrived. I was jittery to be honest as I had taken a gamble and if would not click, I knew I was standing alone in the firing line. First day was a humdinger. All our frontline staff had taken to sales like duck to water. The average ticket size per customer started showing very high growths as all of them focussed on selling the highest price products to get the highest incentive. Next forty days was mayhem with staff going berserk with calculations of how much they have earned. It was a ticket to happiness and fantastic festival period which they could enjoy with their family. Even the unionised staff in Kolkata who hardly moved their fingers at work were busy calling, cajoling, upselling to customers. I have never witnessed such passion and intensity of sales pitches ever in my life and many of those customer propositions could have surely gone into shark tank.

We ended the Durga Puja period with a Like for Like growth of 12%. From a double digit negative Like for Like to positive 12% was a swing of nearly 25%, which is unheard and unthinkable in brick and mortar retail. One of a very senior leader of Pantaloons commented, "There are turnarounds but this was the grandmother of all, no one else could have pulled it off".

Moral of the story: Fear of failing is worse than actual failure which can be turned around by unshackling the basic instinct of rational human beings which in economic terms means providing opportunity to create more goodness for them.